THE

# RUDDER GRANGERS ABROAD

## AND OTHER STORIES

THE

# RUDDER GRANGERS
# ABROAD

*AND OTHER STORIES*

BY

FRANK R. STOCKTON

NEW YORK
CHARLES SCRIBNER'S SONS
1891

# CONTENTS.

# EUPHEMIA AMONG THE PELICANS.

THE sun shone warm and soft, as it shines in winter time in the semi-tropics. The wind blew strong, as it blows whenever and wherever it listeth. Seven pelicans labored slowly through the air. A flock of ducks rose from the surface of the river. A school of mullet, disturbed by a shark, or some other unscrupulous pursuer, sprang suddenly out of the water just before us, and fell into it again like the splashing of a sudden shower.

I lay upon the roof of the cabin of a little yacht. Euphemia stood below, her feet upon the mess-chest, and her elbows resting on the edge of the cabin roof. A sudden squall would have unshipped her; still, if one would be happy, there are risks that must be assumed. At the open entrance of the cabin, busily writing on a hanging-shelf that served as a table, sat a Paying Teller. On the high box which during most of the day covered our stove was a little lady, writing in a note-book. On the forward deck, at the foot of the mast, sat a young man in a state of placidness. His feet stuck out on the bowsprit, while his mildly contemplative eyes went forth unto the roundabout.

1

At the tiller stood our guide and boatman, his sombre eye steady on the south-by-east. Around the horizon of his countenance there spread a dark and six-days' beard, like a slowly rising thunder-cloud; ever and anon there was a gleam of white teeth, like a bright break in the sky, but it meant nothing. During all our trip, the sun never shone in that face. It never stormed, but it was always cloudy. But he was the best boatman on those waters, and when he stood at the helm we knew we sailed secure. We wanted a man familiar with storms and squalls, and if this familiarity had developed into facial sympathy, it mattered not. We could attend to our own sunshine. At his feet sat humbly his boy of twelve, whom we called "the crew." He was making fancy knots in a bit of rope. This and the occupation of growing up were the only labors in which he willingly engaged.

Euphemia and I had left Rudder Grange, to spend a month or two in Florida, and we were now on a little sloop-yacht on the bright waters of the Indian River. It must not be supposed that, because we had a Paying Teller with us, we had set up a floating bank. With this Paying Teller, from a distant State, we had made acquaintance on our first entrance into Florida. He was travelling in what Euphemia called "a group," which consisted of his wife, — the little lady with the note-book, — the contemplative young man on the forward deck, and himself.

This Paying Teller had worked so hard and so rapidly at his business for several years, and had paid out so much of his health and strength, that it was necessary for him to receive large deposits of these essentials before he could go to work again. But the peculiar habits of his profession never left him. He was continually paying out something. If you presented a conversational check to him in the way of a remark, he would, figuratively speaking, immediately jump to his little window and proceed to cash it, sometimes astonishing you by the amount of small change he would spread out before you.

When he heard of our intention to cruise on Indian River he wished to join his group to our party, and as he was a good fellow we were glad to have him do so. His wife had been, or was still, a school-teacher. Her bright and cheerful face glistened with information.

The contemplative young man was a distant connection of the Teller, and his first name being Quincy, was commonly called Quee. If he had wanted to know any of the many things the little teacher wished to tell he would have been a happy youth; but his contemplation seldom crystallized into a knowledge of what he did want to know.

" And how can I," she once said to Euphemia and myself, "be expected ever to offer him any light when he can never bring himself to actually roll up a question ? "

This was said while I was rolling a cigarette.

The group was greatly given to writing in journals, and making estimates. Euphemia and I did little of this, as it was our holiday, but it was often pleasant to see the work going on. The business in which the Paying Teller was now engaged was the writing of his journal, and his wife held a pencil in her kidded fingers and a little blank-book on her knees.

This was our first day upon the river.

"Where are we?" asked Euphemia. "I know we are on the Indian River, but where is the Indian River?"

"It is here," I said.

"But where is here?" reiterated Euphemia.

"There are only three places in the world," said the teacher, looking up from her book, — "here, there, and we don't know where. Every spot on earth is in one or the other of those three places."

"As far as I am concerned," said Euphemia, "the Indian River is in the last place."

"Then we must hasten to take it out," said the teacher, and she dived into the cabin, soon reappearing with a folding map of Florida. "Here," she said, "do you see that wide river running along part of the Atlantic coast of the State, and extending down as far as Jupiter Inlet? That is Indian River, and we are on it. Its chief characteristics are that it is not a river, but an arm of the sea, and that it is full of fish."

"It seems to me to be so full," said I, "that there is not room for them all — that is, if we are to judge by the way the mullet jump out."

"I think," said the teacher, making a spot with her pencil on the map, "that just now we are about here."

"It is the first time," said Euphemia, "that I ever looked upon an unknown region on the map, and felt I was there."

Our plans for travel and living were very simple. We had provided ourselves on starting with provisions for several weeks, and while on the river we cooked and ate on board our little vessel. When we reached Jupiter Inlet we intended to go into camp. Every night we anchored near the shore. Euphemia and I occupied the cabin of the boat; a tent was pitched on shore for the Teller and his wife; there was another tent for the captain and his boy, and this was shared by the contemplative young man.

Our second night on the river was tinged with incident. We had come to anchor near a small settlement, and our craft had been moored to a rude wharf. About the middle of the night a wind-storm arose, and Euphemia and I were awakened by the bumping of the boat against the wharf-posts. Through the open end of the cabin I could see that the night was very dark, and I began to consider the question whether or not it would be necessary for me to get up, much preferring, however, that the wind should go down. Before I had made up my mind we heard a step on the cabin above us, and then a quick and hurried tramping. I put my head out of the little window by me, and cried —

"Who's there?"

The voice of the boatman replied out of the darkness: —

"She'll bump herself to pieces against this pier! I'm going to tow you out into the stream." And so he cast us loose, and getting into the little boat which was fastened to our stern, and always followed us as

a colt its mother, he towed us far out into the stream.
There he anchored us, and rowed away. The bumps
now ceased, but the wind still blew violently, the
waves ran high, and the yacht continually wobbled up
and down, tugging and jerking at her anchor. Neither
of us was frightened, but we could not sleep.

"I know nothing can happen," said Euphemia, "for
he would not have left us here if everything had not
been all right, but one might as well try to sleep in a
corn-popper as in this bed."

After a while the violent motion ceased, and there
was nothing but a gentle surging up and down.

"I am so glad the wind has lulled," said Euphemia,
from the other side of the centre-board partition which
partially divided the cabin.

Although I could still hear the wind blowing strongly
outside, I too was glad that its force had diminished
so far that we felt no more the violent jerking that
had disturbed us, and I soon fell asleep.

In the morning, when I awoke, I saw that the sun
was shining brightly, and that a large sea-grape bush
was hanging over our stern. I sprang out of bed, and
found that we had run, stern foremost, upon a sandy
beach. About forty feet away, upon the shore, stood
two 'possums, gazing with white, triangular faces
upon our stranded craft. Except these, and some
ducks swimming near us, with seven pelicans flying
along on the other side of the river, there was no sign
of life within the range of my sight. I was not long
in understanding the situation. It had not been the
lulling of the storm, but the parting of our cable which

had caused the uneasy jerking of our little yacht to cease. We had been blown I knew not how far down the river, for the storm had come from the north, and had stranded I knew not where. Taking out my pocket-compass I found that we were on the eastern shore of the river, and that the wind had changed completely, and was now blowing, not very strong, from the southeast. I made up my mind what must be done. We were probably far from the settlement and the rest of the party, and we must go back. The wind was in our favor, and I knew I could sail the boat. I had never sailed a boat in my life, and was only too glad to have the opportunity, untrammelled by any interference.

I awoke Euphemia and told her what had happened. The two 'possums stood upon the shore, and listened to our coversation. Euphemia was much impressed by the whole affair, and for a time said nothing.

"We must sail her back, I suppose," she remarked at length, "but do you know how to start her?"

"The hardest thing to do is to get her off the beach," I answered, "but I think I can do that."

I rolled up my trousers, and with bare feet jumped out upon the sand. The two 'possums retired a little, but still watched my proceedings. After a great deal of pushing and twisting and lifting, I got the yacht afloat, and then went on board to set the sail. After much pulling and tugging, and making myself very warm, I hoisted the main-sail. I did not trouble myself about the jib, one sail being enough for me to begin with. As the wind was blowing in the direction in which we wished to go, I let the sail out until it stood nearly at right angles with the vessel, and was delighted to see that we immediately began to move through the water. I took the tiller, and steered gradually toward the middle of the river. The wind blew steadily, and the yacht moved bravely on. I was as proud as a man drawn by a conquered lion, and as happy as one who did not know that conquered lions may turn and rend. Sometimes the vessel rolled so much that the end of the boom skimmed the surface of the water, and sometimes the sail gave a little jerk and flap, but I saw no necessity for changing our course, and kept our bow pointed steadily up the river. I was delighted that the direction of the wind enabled me to sail with what might be called a horizontal deck. Of course, as the boatman afterward informed me, this was the most dangerous way I could steer, for if the sail should suddenly "jibe," there would be no knowing what would happen. Euphemia sat near me, perfectly placid and cheerful, and her absolute trust in me gave me renewed confidence and pleasure. "There is one great comfort," she remarked, as she sat gazing into the water, — "if anything should happen to the boat, we can get out and walk."

There was force in this remark, for the Indian River in some of its widest parts is very shallow, and we could now plainly see the bottom, a few feet below us.

"Is that the reason you have seemed so trustful and content?" I asked.

"That is the reason," said Euphemia.

On we went and on, the yacht seeming sometimes a little restive and impatient, and sometimes rolling more than I could see any necessity for, but still it proceeded. Euphemia sat in the shadow of the cabin, serene and thoughtful, and I, holding the tiller steadily amidship, leaned back and gazed up into the clear blue sky.

In the midst of my gazing there came a shock that knocked the tiller out of my hand. Euphemia sprang to her feet and screamed; there were screams and shouts on the other side of the sail, which seemed to be wrapping itself about some object I could not see. In an instant another mast beside our own appeared above the main-sail, and then a man with a red face jumped on the forward deck. With a quick, determined air, and without saying a word, or seeming to care for my permission, he proceeded to lower our sail; then he stepped up on top of the cabin, and looking down at me, inquired what in thunder I was trying to do.

I made no answer, but looked steadily before me. Now that the sail was down, I could see what had happened. I had collided with a yacht which we had seen before. It was larger than ours, and contained a grandfather and a grandmother, a father and a mother, several aunts, and a great many children. They had started on the river the same day as ourselves, but did not intend to take so extended a trip as ours was to be. The whole party was now in the greatest confusion. I did not understand what they said, nor did I attend to it. I was endeavoring, for myself, to

grasp the situation. Euphemia was calling to me
from the cabin, into which she had retreated; the
man was still talking to me from the cabin roof, and
the people in the other boat were vociferating and
screaming; but I paid no attention to any one until I
had satisfied myself that nothing serious had happened. I had not run into them head on, but had
come up diagonally, and the side of our bow had
struck the side of their stern. The collision, as I
afterward learned, had happened in this wise: I had
not seen the other boat because, lying back as I had
been, the sail concealed her from me, and they had not
seen us because their boatman was in the forward
part of their cabin, collecting materials for breakfast,
and the tiller was left in charge of one of the boys,
who, like all the rest of his party who sat outside, had
discreetly turned his back to the sun.

The grandfather stood up in the stern. He wore a
black silk hat, and carried a heavy grape-vine cane.
Unsteadily balancing himself on his legs, and shaking
his cane at me, he cried: —

"What is the meaning of this, sir? Are you trying to drown a whole family, sir?"

"If he'd run his bowsprit in among you," said the
boatman from the cabin roof, "he'd 'a' killed a lot of
you before you'd been drowned."

Euphemia screamed to me to come to her; the
father was standing on his cabin roof, shouting something to me; the women in the other boat were violently talking among themselves; some of the little
children were crying; the girls were hanging to the

ladies, and all the boys were clambering on board our
boat. It was a time of great excitement, and something must be instantly said by me. My decision was
quick.

"Have you any tea?" I said, addressing the old
gentleman.

"Tea!" he roared. "What do you mean by that?"

"We have plenty of coffee on board," I answered,
"but some of our party can't drink it. If you have
any tea, I should like to borrow some. I can send it
to you when we reach a store."

From every person of the other party came, as in a
chorus, the one word, "Tea?" And Euphemia put
her pale face out of the cabin, and said, in a tone of
wondering inquiry, "Tea?"

"Did you bang into us this way to borrow tea?"
roared the old gentleman.

"I did not intend, of course, to strike you so hard,"
I said, "and I am sorry I did so, but I should like to
borrow some tea."

Euphemia whispered to me: —

"We have tea."

I looked at her, and she locked her lips.

"Of course we can give you some tea, if you want
some," said the red-faced boatman, "but I never heerd
of a thing like this since I was first born, nor ever shall
again, I hope."

"I don't want you to give me any tea," I said.
"I shall certainly return it, and a very little will do —
just a handful."

The two boats had not drifted apart, for the father,

standing on the cabin roof, had held tightly to our rigging, and the boatman, still muttering, went on board his vessel to get the tea. He brought it, wrapped in a piece of a newspaper.

"Here comes your man," he said, pointing to a little boat which was approaching us. "We told him we'd look out for you, but we didn't think you'd come smashing into us like this."

In a few moments our boatman had pulled alongside, his face full of a dark inquiry. He looked at me for authoritative information.

"I came here," I said to him, "after tea."

"Before breakfast, I should say!" cried the old gentleman. And every one of his party burst out laughing.

Much was now said, chiefly by the party of the other part, but our boatman paid little attention to any of it. The boys scrambled on board their own vessel. We pushed apart, hoisted sail, and were soon speeding away.

"Good bye!" shouted the father, a genial man. "Let us know if you want any more groceries, and we'll send them to you."

For six days from our time of starting we sailed down the Indian River. Sometimes the banks were miles apart, and sometimes they were very near each other; sometimes we would come upon a solitary house, or little cluster of dwellings; and then there would be many, many miles of wooded shore before another human habitation was to be seen. Inland, to the west, stretched a vast expanse of lonely forest where panthers, bears, and wild-cats prowled. To the east lay a long strip of land, through whose tall palmettoes came the roar of the great ocean. The blue sky sparkled over us every day; now and then we met a little solitary craft; countless water-fowl were scattered about on the surface of the stream; a school of mullet was usually jumping into the air; an alligator might sometimes be seen steadily swimming across the river, with only his nose and back exposed; and nearly always, either to the right or to the left, going north or going south, were seven pelicans, slowly flopping through the air.

A portion of the river, far southward, called "The Narrows," presented a very peculiar scene. The banks were scarcely fifty feet apart, and yet there were no banks. The river was shut in to the right by the inland shore, and to the left by a far-reaching island, and yet there was no inland shore, nor any island to the left. On either side were great forests of mangrove trees, standing tiptoe on their myriad down-dropping roots, each root midleg in the water. As far as we could see among the trees, there was no sign of ground of any kind — nothing but a grotesque network of roots, on which the forest stood. In this green-bordered avenue of water, which extended nine or ten miles, the thick foliage shut out the breeze, and our boatman was obliged to go ahead in his little boat and tow us along.

"There are Indians out West," said Euphemia, as she sat gazing into the mangroves, "who live on roots, but I don't believe they could live on these. The pappooses would certainly fall through."

At Jupiter Inlet, about a hundred and fifty miles from our point of starting, we went into camp, in which delightful condition we proposed to remain for a week or more. There was no trouble whatever in finding a suitable place for a camp. The spot selected was a point of land swept by cool breezes, with a palmetto forest in the rear of it. On two sides of the point stretched the clear waters of the river, while half a mile to the east was Jupiter Inlet, on each side of which rolled and tumbled the surf of the Atlantic. About a mile away was Jupiter Light-house, the only human habitation within twenty miles. We built a palmetto hut for a kitchen; we set up the tents in a permanent way; we constructed a little pier for the yacht; we built a wash-stand, a table, and a bench. And then, considering that we had actually gone into camp, we got out our fishing-lines.

Fishing was to be the great work here. Near the Inlet, through which the waters of the ocean poured into and out of our river, on a long, sandy beach, we stood in line, two or three hours every day except Sunday, and fished. Such fishing we had never imagined! — there were so many fishes, and they were so big. The Paying Teller had never fished in his life before he came to Florida. He had tried at St. Augustine, with but little success. "If the sport had been to chuck fish into the river," he had said, "that would be more in my line of business; but getting them out of it did not seem to suit me." But here it was quite a different thing. It was a positive delight to him, he said, to be obliged so often to pay out his line.

One day, when tired of struggling with gamy blue-fish and powerful cavalios (if that is the way to spell it), I wound up my line, and looked about to see what the others were doing. The Paying Teller stood near, on tiptoe, as usual, with his legs wide apart, his hat thrown back, his eyes flashing over the water, and his right arm stretched far out, ready for a jerk. Quee was farther along the beach. He had just landed a fish, and was standing gazing meditatively upon it as it lay upon the sand. The hook was still in its mouth, and every now and then he would give the line a little pull, as if to see if there really was a connection between it and the fish. Then he would stand a little longer, and meditate a little more, still looking alternately at the line and the fish. Having made up his mind, at last, that the two things must be separated, he kneeled down upon his flopping prize and proceeded meditatively to extract the hook. The teacher was struggling at her line. Hand over hand she pulled it in. As it came nearer and nearer, her fish swam wildly from side to side, making the tightened line fairly hiss as it swept through the water. But still she pulled and pulled, until, red and breathless, she landed her prize upon the sand.

"Hurrah!" shouted the Paying Teller. "That's the biggest blue-fish yet!" But he did not come to take the fish from the hook. He was momentarily expecting a bite.

Euphemia was not to be seen. This did not surprise me, as she frequently gave up fishing long before the others, and went to stroll upon the sea-beach, a few hundred yards away. She was fond of fishing, but it soon tired her. "If you want to know what it is like," she wrote to a friend in the North, "just tie a long string around your boy Charlie, and try to haul him out of the back yard into the house."

But Euphemia was not upon the sea-beach to-day. I walked a mile or so along the sand, but did not find her. She had gone around the little bluff to our shark-line. This was a long rope, like a clothes-line, with a short chain at the end and a great hook, which was baited with a large piece of fish. It was thrown out every day, the land end tied to a stout stake driven into the sand, and the whole business given into the charge of "the crew," who was to report if a shark should bite. But to-day the little rascal had wandered away, and Euphemia was managing the line.

"I thought I would try to catch a shark all by my-self," she said. "I wonder if there's one on the hook now. Would you mind feeling the line?"

I laughed as I took the rope from her hand.

"If you had a shark on the hook, my dear," said I, "you would have no doubt upon the subject."

"It would be a splendid thing to catch the first one," she said, "and there must be lots of them in here, for we have seen their back fins so often."

I was about to answer this remark when I began to walk out into the water. I did not at the time know exactly why I did this, but it seemed as if some one had taken me by the hand and was leading me into the depths. But the water splashing above my ankles and a scream from Euphemia made me drop the line, which immediately spun out to its full length, making the stake creak and move in the sand.

"Goodness gracious!" cried Euphemia, her face pale as the beach. "Isn't it horrible? We've got one!"

"Horrible!" I cried. "Didn't you want to get one?" and seizing the axe, which lay near by, I drove the stake deep down into the sand. "Now it will hold him!" I cried. "He can't pull that out!"

"But how are we to pull him in?" exclaimed Euphemia. "This line is as tight as a guitar-string."

This was true. I took hold of the rope, but could make no impression on it. Suddenly it slackened in my hand.

"Hurrah!" I cried, "we may have him yet! But we must play him."

"Play him!" exclaimed Euphemia. "You can never play a huge creature like that. Let me go and call some of the others to help."

"No, no!" I said. "Perhaps we can do it all by ourselves. Wind the line quickly around the top of the stake as I pull it in."

Euphemia knelt down and rapidly wound several yards of the slack cord around the stake. In a few moments it tightened again, jerking itself out of my hand.

"There, now!" said Euphemia. "He is off again! You can never haul him in, now."

"Just wait," I said. "When he finds that he cannot break away he rushes toward shore, trying to bite the line above the chain. Then I must haul it in and you must wind it up. If you and I and the shark continue to act in this way, perhaps, after a time, we may get him into shallow water. But don't scream or shout. I don't want the others to know anything about it."

Sure enough, in a minute or two the line slackened again, when it was rapidly drawn in and wound around the stake.

"There he is!" exclaimed Euphemia. "I can see him just under the water, out there."

The dark form of the shark, appearing at first like the shadow of a little cloud, could be seen near the surface, about fifteen yards away. Then his back fin rose, his tail splashed violently for an instant, and he disappeared. Again the line was loosened, and again the slack was hauled in and wound up. This was repeated, I don't know how many times, when suddenly the shark in his desperation rushed into shallow water and grounded himself. He would have floundered off in a few moments, however, had we not quickly tightened the line. Now we could see him plainly. He was eight or nine feet long and struggled violently, exciting Euphemia so much that it was only by clapping her hand over her mouth that she prevented herself from screaming. I would have pulled the shark farther in shore, but this was impossible, and it was needless to expect him to move himself into shallower water. So, quickly rolling up my trousers, I seized the axe and waded in toward the floundering creature.

"You needn't be afraid to go right up to him," said

Euphemia. "So long as he don't turn over on his back he can't bite you."

I had heard this bit of natural history before, but, nevertheless, I went no nearer to the shark than was necessary in order to whack him over the head with the axe. This I did several times, with such effect that he soon became a dead shark.

When I came out triumphant, Euphemia seized me in her arms and kissed me.

"This is perfectly splendid!" she said. "Who can show as big a fish as this one? None of the others can ever crow over you again."

"Until one of them catches a bigger shark," I said.

"Which none of them ever will," said Euphemia, decidedly. "It isn't in them."

The boatman was now seen approaching in his boat to take the party back to camp, and the "crew," having returned to his duty, was sent off in a state of absolute amazement to tell the others to come and look at our prize. Our achievement certainly created a sensation. Even the boatman could find no words to express his astonishment. He waded in and fastened a rope to the shark's tail, and then we all took hold and hauled the great fish ashore.

"What is the good of it now you have got it?" asked Quee.

"Glory is some good!" exclaimed Euphemia.

"And I'm going to have you a belt made from a strip of its skin," I said.

This seemed to Euphemia a capital idea. She would be delighted to have such a trophy of our deed, and

the boatman was set to work to cut a suitable strip
from the fish. And this belt, having been properly
tanned, lined, and fitted with buckles, is now one of
her favorite adornments, and cost, I am bound to add,
about three times as much as any handsome leathern
belt to be bought in the stores.

Every day the Paying Teller, his wife, and Quee
carefully set down in their note-books the weight of
fish each individual had caught, with all necessary
details and specifications relating thereunto; every
day we wandered on the beach, or explored the trop-
ical recesses of the palmetto woods; every evening
the boatman rowed over to the light-house to have a
bit of gossip, and to take thither the fish we did not
need; every day the sun was soft and warm, and the
sky was blue; and every morning, going oceanward,
and every evening, going landward, seven pelicans
flew slowly by our camp.

My greatest desire at this time was to shoot a
pelican, to have him properly prepared, and to take
him to Rudder Grange, where, suitably set up, with
his wings spread out, full seven feet from tip to tip,
he would be a grand trophy and reminder of these
Indian River days. This was the reason why, nearly
every morning and every evening, I took a shot at
these seven pelicans. But I never hit one of them.
We had only a shot-gun, and the pelicans flew at a
precautionary distance; but, being such big birds,
they always looked to me much nearer than they
were. Euphemia earnestly desired that I should
have a pelican, and although she always wished I

should hit one of these, she was always glad when I did not.

"Think how mournful it would be," she said, "if they should take their accustomed flights, morning and evening, with one of their number missing."

"Repeating Wordsworth's verses, I suppose," remarked the little teacher.

I had been disappointed in the number of pelicans we had seen. I knew that Florida was one of the homes of the pelican, and I had not expected to see these birds merely in small detachments. But our boatman assured me that on our return trip he would give me a chance of seeing and shooting as many pelicans as I could desire. We would touch at Pelican Island, which was inhabited entirely by these birds, and whence the parties of seven were evidently sent out.

When we had had all the fishing we wanted, we broke up our camp, and started northward. We had all been very happy and contented during our ten days' sojourn in this delightful place; but when at last our departure was determined upon, the Paying Teller became possessed with a wild desire to go, go, go. There was some reason, never explained nor fully expressed, why no day, hour, minute, or second should be lost in speeding to the far Northwest. The boatman, too, impelled by what impulse I know not, seemed equally anxious to get home. As for the Paying Teller's "group," it always did exactly as he wished. Therefore, although Euphemia and I would have been glad to linger here and there upon our

homeward way, we could not gainsay the desire of
the majority of the party, and consequently we sailed
northward as fast as wind and sometimes oars would
take us.

Only one cause for delay seemed tolerable to the
Paying Teller. This was to stop at every post-office.
We had received but one mail while in camp, which
had been brought in a sail-boat from an office twenty
miles away. But the Paying Teller had given and
written the most intricate and complex directions for
the retention or forwarding of his mail to every postmaster in the country we had passed through, and
these directions, as we afterward found, had so puzzled and unsettled the minds of these postmasters that
for several weeks his letters had been moving like
shuttlecocks up and down the St. John's and Indian
rivers — never stopping anywhere, never being delivered, but crossing and recrossing each other as if they
were imbued with their owner's desire to go, go, go.
Some of the post-offices where we stopped were lonely
little buildings with no other habitation near. These
we usually found shut up, being opened only on mail-
days, and in such cases nothing could be done but to
slip a protesting postal into the little slit in the wall
apparently intended for letters. Whether these pos-
tals were eaten by rats or read by the P.M.'s, we
never discovered. Wherever an office was found open,
we left behind us an irate postmaster breathing all
sorts of contemplated vengeance upon the disturbers
of his peace. We heard of letters that had been sent
north and sent south, but there never were any at the

particular place where we happened to be, and I suppose that the accumulated mail of the Paying Teller may for several years drop gradually upon him through the meshes of the Dead-Letter Office.

There were a great many points of interest which we had passed on our downward trip, the boatman assuring us that, with the wind we had, and which might cease at any moment, the great object was to reach Jupiter as soon as possible, and that we would stop at the interesting places on the way up. But now the wind, according to his reasoning, made it necessary that we should again push forward as fast as we could; and, as I said before, the irresistible attraction of the Northwest so worked upon the Paying Teller that he was willing to pause nowhere, during the daytime, but at a post-office. At one place, however, I was determined to land. This was Pelican Island. The boatman, paying no attention to his promise to stop here and give me an opportunity to shoot one of these birds, declared, when near the place, that it would never do, with such a wind, to drop anchor for a trifle like a pelican. The Paying Teller and Quee also strongly objected to a stop; and, while the teacher had a great desire to investigate the subject of ornithology, especially when exemplified by such a subject as a pelican, she felt herself obliged to be loyal to her "group," and so quietly gave her voice to go on. But I, supported by Euphemia, remained so firm that we anchored a short distance from Pelican Island.

None of the others had any desire to go ashore, and

so I, with the gun and Euphemia, took the boat and rowed to the island. While we were here the others determined to sail to the opposite side of the river to look for a little post-office, the existence of which the boatman had not mentioned until it had been determined to make this stoppage here.

As we approached the island we saw hundreds of pelicans, some flying about, some sitting on trunks and branches of dead trees, and some waddling about on the shore.

"You might as well shoot two of them," said Euphemia, "and then we will select the better one to take to Rudder Grange."

The island was very boggy and muddy, and, before I had found a good place to land, and had taken up the gun from the bow of the boat, every pelican in sight took wing and flew away. I stood up and fired both barrels at the retreating flock. They swerved and flew oceanward, but not one of them fell. I helped Euphemia on shore, and then, gun in hand, I made my way as well as I could to the other end of the island. There might be some deaf old fellows left who had not made up their minds to fly. The ground was very muddy, and drift-wood and underbrush obstructed my way. Still, I pressed on, and went nearly half around the island, finding, however, not a single pelican.

Soon I heard Euphemia's voice, calling loud. She seemed to be about the centre of the island, and I ran toward her.

"I've got one!" I heard her cry, before I came in

sight of her.  She was sitting at the root of a crooked, dead tree.  In front of her she held, one hand grasping each leg, what seemed to me to be an ungainly and wingless goose.  All about her the ground was soft and boggy.  Her clothes were muddy, her face was red, and the creature she held was struggling violently.

"What on earth have you got?" I exclaimed, approaching as near as I could, "and how did you get out there?"

"Don't you come any closer!" she cried.  "You'll sink up to your waist!  I got here by treading on the little hummocks and holding on to that dead branch; but don't you take hold of it, for you'll break it off, and then I can't get back."

"But what is that thing?" I repeated.

"It's a young pelican," she replied.  "I found a lot of nests on the ground over there, and this was in one of them.  I chased it all about, until it flopped out here and hid itself on the other side of this tree.  Then I came out quietly and caught it.  But how am I going to get it to you?"

This seemed, indeed, a problem.  Euphemia declared that she needed both hands to work her way back by the means of the long, horizontal limb which had assisted her passage to the place where she sat, and she also needed both hands to hold her prize.  It was likewise plain that I could not get to her.  Indeed, I could not see how her light steps had taken her over the soft and marshy ground that lay between us.  I suggested that she should throw the pelican to me.  This she declined to do.

"I could never throw it so far," she said, "and it would surely get away. I don't want to lose this pelican, for I believe it is the last one on the island. If there are other young ones, they have scuttled off by this time, and I should dreadfully hate to go back to the yacht without any pelican at all."

"I don't call that much of one," I said.

"It's a real pelican for all that," she replied, "and about as curious a bird as I ever saw. Its wings won't stretch out seven feet, to be sure."

"About seven inches," I suggested.

"But it is a great deal easier to carry a young one like this," she persisted, "and I expect a baby pelican is a much more uncommon sight in the North than a grown one."

"No doubt of it," I said. "We must keep him now you've got him. Can't you kill him?"

"I've no way of killing him," returned Euphemia. "I wonder if you could shoot him if I were to hold him out."

This, with a shot-gun, I positively declined to do. Even if I had had a rifle, I suggested that she might swerve. For a few moments we remained nonplussed. I could not get to Euphemia at all, and she could not get to me unless she released her bird, and this she was determined not to do.

"Euphemia," I said, presently, "the ground seems hard a little way in front of you. If you step over there, I will go out on this strip, which seems pretty solid. Then I'll be near enough to you for you to swing the bird to me, and I'll catch hold of him."

Euphemia arose and did as I told her, and we soon found ourselves about six feet apart. She took the bird by one leg and swung it toward me. With outstretched arm I caught it by the other foot, but as I did so I noticed that Euphemia was growing shorter, and also felt myself sinking in the bog. Instantly I entreated Euphemia to stand perfectly still, for, if we struggled or moved, there was no knowing into what more dreadful depths we might get. Euphemia obeyed me, and stood quite still, but I could feel that she clutched the pelican with desperate vigor.

"How much farther down do you think we shall sink?" she asked, her voice trembling a little.

"Not much farther," I said. "I am sure there is firm ground beneath us, but it will not do to move. If we should fall down, we might not be able to get up again."

"How glad I am," she said, "that we are not entirely separated, even if it is only a baby pelican that joins us!"

"Indeed, I am glad!" I said, giving the warm pressure to the pelican's leg that I would have given to Euphemia's hand, if I could have reached her. Euphemia looked up at me so confidently that I could but believe that in some magnetic way that pressure had been transmitted through the bird.

"Do you think they will come back?" she said, directly.

"Oh, yes," I replied, "there's no manner of doubt of that."

"They'll be dreadfully cross," she said.

"I shouldn't wonder," I replied. "But it makes very little difference to me whether they are or not."

"It ought to make a difference to you," said Euphemia. "They might injure us very much."

"If they tried anything of the kind," I replied, "they'd find it worse for them than for us."

"That is boasting," said Euphemia, a little reproachfully, "and it does not sound like you."

I made no answer to this, and then she asked: —

"What do you think they will do when they come?"

"I think they will put a plank out here and pull us out."

Euphemia looked at me an instant, and then her eyes filled with tears.

"Oh, dear!" she exclaimed, "it's dreadful! You know they couldn't do it. Your mind is giving way!"

She sobbed, and I could feel the tremor run through the pelican.

"What do you mean?" I cried, anxiously. "My mind giving way?"

"Yes — yes," she sobbed. "If you were in your right senses — you'd never think — that pelicans could bring a plank."

I looked at her in astonishment.

"Pelicans!" I exclaimed. "Did you think I meant the pelicans were coming back?"

"Of course," she said. "That's what I was asking you about."

"I wasn't thinking of pelicans at all," I answered. "I was talking of the people in the yacht."

Euphemia looked at me, and then the little pelican between us began to shake violently as we laughed.

"I know people sometimes do lose their minds when they get into great danger," she said, apologetically.

"Hello!" came a voice from the water. "What are you laughing about?"

"Come and see," I shouted back, "and perhaps you will laugh, too."

The three men came; they had to wade ashore; and when they came they laughed. They brought a plank, and with a good deal of trouble they drew us out, but Euphemia would not let go of her leg of the little pelican until she was sure I had a tight hold of mine.

Day after day we now sailed northward, until we reached the little town at which we had embarked. Here we discarded our blue flannels and three half-grown beards, and slowly made our way through woods and lakes and tortuous streams to the upper waters of the St. John's. In this region the population of the river shores seemed to consist entirely of alligators, in which monsters Euphemia was greatly interested. But she seldom got a near view of one, for the sportsmen on our little steamer blazed away at every alligator as soon as it came into distant sight; and, although the ugly creatures were seldom hit, they made haste to tumble into the water or disappear among the tall reeds. Euphemia was very much annoyed at this.

"I shall never get a good close look at an alligator at all," she said. "I am going to speak to the captain."

The captain, a big, good-natured man, listened to her, and entirely sympathized with her.

"Tom," said he to the pilot, "when you see another big 'gator on shore, don't sing out to nobody, but call me, and slow up."

It was not long before chocolate-colored Tom called to the captain, and rang the bell to lessen speed.

"Gentlemen," said the captain, walking forward to the group of sportsmen, "there's a big 'gator ahead there, but don't none of you fire at him. He's copyrighted."

The men with the guns did not understand him, but none of them fired, and Euphemia and the other ladies soon had the satisfaction of seeing an enormous alligator lying on the bank, within a dozen yards of the boat. The great creature raised its head, and looked at us in apparent amazement at not being shot at. Then, probably considering that we did not know the customs of the river, or were out of ammunition, he slowly slipped away among the reeds with an air as if, like Mr. Turveydrop, he had done his duty in showing himself, and if we did not take advantage of it, it was no affair of his.

"If we only had a fellow like that for a trophy!" ejaculated Euphemia.

"He'd do very well for a trophy," I answered, "but if, in order to get him, I had to hold him by one leg while you held him by another, I should prefer a baby pelican."

Our trip down the St. John's met with no obstacles except those occasioned by the Paying Teller's return tickets. He had provided himself and his group with all sorts of return tickets from the various points he had expected to visit in Florida. These were good only on particular steamboats, and could be used only to go from one particular point to another. Fortunately he had lost several of them, but there were enough left to give us a good deal of trouble. We did not wish to break up the party, and consequently we embarked and disembarked whenever the Paying Teller's group did so; and thus, in time, we all reached that widespread and sandy city which serves for the gate of Florida.

From here, the Paying Teller and his group, with complicated tickets, the determinate scope and purpose of which no one man living could be expected to understand, hurried wildly toward the far Northwest; while we, in slower fashion, returned to Rudder Grange.

There, in a place of honor over the dining-room door, stands the baby pelican, its little flippers wide outstretched.

"How often I think," Euphemia sometimes says, "of that moment of peril, when the only actual bond of union between us was that little pelican!"

# THE RUDDER GRANGERS IN ENGLAND.

IT was mainly due to Pomona that we went to Europe at all. For years Euphemia and I had been anxious to visit the enchanted lands on the other side of the Atlantic, but the obstacles had always been very great, and the matter had been indefinitely postponed. Pomona and Jonas were still living with us, and their little girl was about two years old. Pomona continued to read a great deal, but her husband's influence had diverted her mind toward works of history and travel, and these she devoured with eager interest. But she had not given up her old fancy for romance. Nearly everything she read was mingled in her mind with Middle Age legends and tales of strange adventure. Euphemia's frequent reference to a trip to Europe had fired Pomona's mind, and she was now more wildly anxious for the journey than any of us. She believed that it would entirely free Jonas from the chills and fever that still seemed to permeate his being. And besides this, what unutterable joy to tread the sounding pavements of those old castles of which she had so often read! Pomona further perceived that my mental and

physical systems required the rest and change of
scene which could be given only by a trip to Europe.
When this impression had been produced upon Euphemia's mind, the matter, to all intents and pur-
poses, was settled. A tenant, who I suspect was
discovered and urged forward by the indefatigable
Pomona, made an application for a year's lease of our
house and farm. In a business view I found I could
make the journey profitable, and there seemed to be
no reason why we should not go, and go now.

It appeared to be accepted as a foregone conclusion
by Euphemia and Pomona that the latter, with her
husband and child, should accompany us; but of this
I could not, at first, see the propriety.

"We shall not want servants on a trip like that," I
said; "and although I like Jonas and Pomona very
much, they are not exactly the people I should prefer
as travelling companions."

"If you think you are going to leave Pomona
behind," said Euphemia, "you are vastly mistaken.
Oceans and continents are free to her, and she will
follow us at a distance if we don't let her go with us.
She was quite content not to go with us to Florida,
but she is just one tingle from head to foot to go to
Europe. We have talked the whole thing over, and I
know that she will be of the greatest possible use and
comfort to me in ever so many ways; and Jonas will
be needed to take care of the baby. Jonas has
money, and they will pay a great part of their own
expenses, and will not cost us much, and you needn't
be afraid that Pomona will make us ashamed of our-

selves, if we happen to be talking to the Dean of Westminster or the Archbishop of Canterbury, by pushing herself into the conversation."

"Indeed," said I, "if we ever happen to be inveigled into a confab with those dignitaries, I hope Pomona will come to the front and take my place."

The only person not entirely satisfied with the proposed journey was Jonas.

"I don't like trapsin' round," said he, "from place to place, and never did. If I could go to some one spot and stay there with the child, while the rest of you made trips, I'd be satisfied, but I don't like keepin' on the steady go."

This plan was duly considered, and the suitability of certain points was discussed. London was not believed sufficiently accessible for frequent return trips; Paris could scarcely be called very central; Naples would not be suitable at all times of the year, and Cairo was a little too far eastward. A number of minor places were suggested, but Jonas announced that he had thought of a capital location, and being eagerly asked to name it, he mentioned Newark, New Jersey.

"I'd feel at home there," he said, "and it's about as central as any place, when you come to look on the map of the world."

But he was not allowed to remain in his beloved New Jersey, and we took him with us to Europe.

We did not, like the rest of the passengers on the steamer, go directly from Liverpool to London, but stopped for a couple of days in the quaint old town of

Chester. "If we don't see it now," said Euphemia, "we never shall see it. When we once start back we shall be raving distracted to get home, and I wouldn't miss Chester for anything."

"There is an old wall there," said the enthusiastic Pomona to her husband, "built by Julius Cæsar before the Romans became Catholics, that you kin walk on all round the town; an' a tower on it which the king of England stood on to see his army defeated, though of course it wasn't put up for that purpose; besides, more old-timenesses which the book tells of than we can see in a week."

"I hope," said Jonas, wearily shifting the child from one arm to the other, "that there'll be some good place there to sit down."

When we reached Chester, we went directly to the inn called "The Gentle Boar," which was selected by Euphemia entirely on account of its name, and we found it truly a quaint and cosey little house. Everything was early English and delightful. The coffee-rooms, the bar-maids, the funny little apartments, the old furniture, and "a general air of the Elizabethan era," as Euphemia remarked.

"I should almost call it Henryan," said Pomona, gazing about her in rapt wonderment.

We soon set out on our expeditions of sight-seeing, but we did not keep together. Euphemia and I made our way to the old cathedral. The ancient verger who took us about the edifice was obliged to show us everything, Euphemia being especially anxious to see the stall in the choir which had belonged to Charles

Kingsley, and was much disturbed to find that under the seat the monks of the fifteenth century had carved the subject of one of Baron Munchausen's most improbable tales.

"Of course," said she, "they did not know that Charles Kingsley was to have this stall, or they would have cut something more appropriate."

"Those old monks 'ad a good deal of fun in them," said the verger, "hand they were particular fond of showing up quarrels between men and their wives, which they could do, you see, without 'urting each other's feelings. These queer carvings are hunder the seats, which turn hup in this way, and I've no doubt they looked at them most of the time they were kneeling on the cold floor saying their long, Latin prayers."

"Yes, indeed!" said Euphemia. "It must have been a great comfort to the poor fellows."

"We went all through that cathedral," exclaimed Pomona, when she came in the next day. "The old virgin took us everywhere."

"Verger," exclaimed Euphemia.

"Well, he looked so like a woman in his long gown," said Pomona, "I don't wonder I mixed him. We put two shillin's in his little box, though one was enough, as I told Jonas, and then he took us round and pointed out all the beautiful carvin's and things on the choir, the transits, and the nave, but when Jonas stopped before the carved figger of the devil chawin' up a sinner, and asked if that was the transit of a knave, the old feller didn't know what he meant. An' then we wandered alone through them ruined cloisters and subterraneal halls, an' old tombstones of the past, till I felt I don't know how. There was a girl in New Jersey who used to put on airs because her family had lived in one place for a hundred years. When I git back I'll laugh that girl to scorn."

After two days of delight in this quaint old town we took the train Londonward. Without consultation Jonas bought tickets for himself and wife, while I bought Euphemia's and mine. Consequently our servants travelled first-class, while we went in a second-class carriage. We were all greatly charmed with the beautiful garden country through which we passed. It was harvest time, and Jonas was much impressed by the large crops gathered from the little fields.

"I might try to do something of that kind when I go back," he afterward said, "but I expect I'd have to dig a little hole for each grain of wheat, and hoe it, and water it, and tie the blade to a stick if it was weakly."

"An' a nice easy time you'd have of it," said Pomona; "for you might plant your wheat field round a stump, and set there, and farm all summer, without once gettin' up."

"And that is Windsor!" exclaimed Euphemia, as we passed within view of that royal castle. "And there lives the Sovereign of our Mother Country!"

I was trying to puzzle out in what relationship to the Sovereign this placed us, when Euphemia continued:—

"I am bound to go to Windsor Castle! I have examined into every style of housekeeping, French flats

and everything, and I must see how the Queen lives.
I expect to get ever so many ideas."

"All right," said I; "and we will visit the royal
stables, too, for I intend to get a new buggy when we
get back."

We determined that on reaching London we would
go directly to lodgings, not only because this was a
more economical way of living, but because it was the
way in which many of Euphemia's favorite heroes and
heroines had lived in London.

"I want to keep house," she said, "in the same way
that Charles and Mary Lamb did. We will toast a
bit of muffin or a potted sprat, and we'll have a hamper of cheese and a tankard of ale, just like those old
English poets and writers."

"I think you are wrong about the hamper of
cheese," I said. "It couldn't have been as much as
that, but I have no doubt we'll have a jolly time."

We got into a four-wheeled cab, Jonas on the seat
with the driver, and the luggage on top. I gave the
man a card with the address of the house to which we
had been recommended. There was a number, the
name of a street, the name of a place, the name of a
square, and initials denoting the quarter of the town.

"It will confuse the poor man dreadfully," said
Euphemia. "It would have been a great deal better
just to have said where the house was."

The man, however, drove to the given address without mistake. The house was small, but as there were
no other lodgers, there was room enough for us.
Euphemia was much pleased with the establishment.

The house was very well furnished, and she had expected to find things old and stuffy, as London lodgings always were in the books she had read.

"But if the landlady will only steal our tea," she said, "it will make it seem more like the real thing."

As we intended to stay some time in London, where I had business to transact for the firm with which I was engaged, we immediately began to make ourselves as much at home as possible. Pomona, assisted by Jonas, undertook at once the work of the house. To this the landlady, who kept a small servant, somewhat objected, as it had been her custom to attend to the wants of her lodgers.

"But what's the good of Jonas an' me bein' here," said Pomona to us, "if we don't do the work? Of course, if there was other lodgers, that would be different, but as there's only our own family, where's the good of that woman and her girl doin' anything?"

And so, as a sort of excuse for her being in Europe, she began to get the table ready for supper, and sent Jonas out to see if there was any place where he could buy provisions. Euphemia and I were not at all certain that the good woman of the house would be satisfied with this state of things; but still, as Jonas and Pomona were really our servants, it seemed quite proper that they should do our work. And so we did not interfere, although Euphemia found it quite sad, she said, to see the landlady standing idly about, gazing solemnly upon Pomona as she dashed from place to place engaged with her household duties.

After we had been in the house for two or three

days, Pomona came into our sitting-room one evening and made a short speech.

"I've settled matters with the woman here," she said, "an' I think you'll like the way I've done it. I couldn't stand her follerin' me about, an' sayin' 'ow they did things in Hingland, while her red-faced girl was a-spendin' the days on the airy steps, a-lookin' through the railin's. 'Now, Mrs. Bowlin',' says I, 'it'll just be the ruin of you an' the death of me if you keep on makin' a picter of yourself like that lonely Indian a-sittin' on a pinnacle in the jographys, watchin' the inroads of civilization, with a locomotive an' a cog-wheel in front, an' the buffalo an' the grisly a-disappearin' in the distance. Now it'll be much better for all of us,' says I, 'if you'll git down from your peak, and try to make up your mind that the world has got to move. Aint there some place where you kin go an' be quiet an' comfortable, an' not a-woundin' your proud spirit a-watchin' me bake hot rolls for breakfast an' sich?' An' then she says she'd begun to think pretty much that way herself, an' that she had a sister a-livin' down in the Sussex Mews, back of Gresham Terrace, Camberwell Square, Hankberry Place, N. W. by N., an' she thought she might as well go there an' stay while we was here. An' so I says that was just the thing, and the sooner done the happier she'd be. An' I went up stairs and helped her pack her trunk, which is a tin one, which she calls her box, an' I got her a cab, an' she's gone."

"What!" I cried; "gone! Has she given up her house entirely to us?"

"For the time bein' she has," answered Pomona, "for she saw very well it was better thus, an' she's comin' every week to git her money, an' to see when we're goin' to give notice. An' the small girl has been sent back to the country."

It was impossible for Euphemia and myself to countenance this outrageous piece of eviction; but in answer to our exclamations of surprise and reproach, Pomona merely remarked that she had done it for the woman's own good, and, as she was perfectly satisfied, she didn't suppose there was any harm done; and, at any rate, it would be "lots nicer" for us. And then she asked Euphemia what she was going to have for breakfast the next morning, so that Jonas could go out to the different mongers and get the things.

"Now," said Euphemia, when Pomona had gone down stairs, "I really feel as if I had a foothold on British soil. It doesn't seem as if 't was quite right, but it is perfectly splendid."

And so it was. From that moment we set up an English Rudder Grange in the establishment which Pomona had thus rudely wrenched, as it were, from the claws of the British Lion. We endeavored to live as far as possible in the English style, because we wanted to try the manners and customs of every country. We had tea for breakfast and ale for luncheon, and we ate shrimps, prawns, sprats, saveloys, and Yarmouth bloaters. We "took in the Times," and, to a certain extent, we endeavored to cultivate the broad vowels. Some of these things we did not like, but we felt bound to allow them a fair trial.

We did not give ourselves up to sight-seeing as we had done at Chester, because now there was plenty of time to see London at our leisure. In the mornings I attended to my business, and in the afternoons Euphemia and I generally went out to visit some of the lions of the grand old city.

Pomona and Jonas also went out whenever a time could be conveniently arranged, which was done nearly every day, for Euphemia was anxious they should see everything. They almost always took their child, and to this Euphemia frequently objected.

"What's the good," she said, "of carrying a baby not two years old to the Tower of London, the British Museum, and the Chapel of Henry VII. ? She can't take any interest in the smothered princes, or the Assyrian remnants. If I am at home, I can look after her as well as not."

"But you see, ma'am," said Pomona, "we don't expect the baby'll ever come over here ag'in, an' when she gits older, I'll tell her all about these things, an' it'll expan' her intelleck a lot more when she feels she's seed 'em all without knowin' it. To be sure, the monnyments of bygone days don't always agree with her; for Jone set her down on the tomb of Chaucer the other day, an' her little legs got as cold as the tomb itself, an' I told him that there was too big a difference between a tomb nigh four hundred years old an' a small baby which don't date back two years, for them to be sot together that way; an' he promised to be more careful after that. He gouged a little piece out of Chaucer's tomb, an' as we went home we bought a copy of the old gentleman's poems, so as we could see what reason there was for keepin' him so long, an' at night I read Jone two of the Canterbury Tales. 'You wouldn't 'a' thought,' says Jone, 'jus' by lookin' at that little piece of plaster, that the old fellow could 'a' got up such stories as them.'"

"What I want to see more'n anything else," said Pomona to us one day, "is a real lord, or some kind of nobleman of high degree. I've allers loved to read about 'em in books, and I'd rather see one close to, than all the tombs and crypts and lofty domes you could rake together; an' I don't want to see 'em neither in the streets, nor yet in a House of Parliament, which aint in session; for there, I don't believe, dressin' in common clothes as they do, that I could tell 'em from other people. What I want is to penetrate into the home of one of 'em, and see him as he really is. It's only there that his noble blood'll come out."

"Pomona," cried Euphemia, in accents of alarm, "don't you try penetrating into any nobleman's home. You will get yourself into trouble, and the rest of us, too."

"Oh, I'm not a-goin' to git you into any trouble, ma'am," said Pomona; "you needn't be afeard of that." And she went about her household duties.

A few days after this, as Euphemia and I were going to the Tower of London in a Hansom cab — and it was one of Euphemia's greatest delights to be bowled over the smooth London pavements in one of these vehicles, with the driver out of sight, and the

horse in front of us just as if we were driving ourselves, only without any of the trouble, and on every
corner one of the names of the streets we had read
about in Dickens and Thackeray, and with the Samp-
son Brasses, and the Pecksniffs, and the Mrs. Gamps,
and the Guppys, and the Sir Leicester Dedlocks, and
the Becky Sharps, and the Pendennises, all walking
about just as natural as in the novels — we were surprised to see Pomona hurrying along the sidewalk
alone. The moment our eyes fell upon her a feeling
of alarm arose within us. Where was she going with
such an intent purpose in her face, and without Jonas?
She was walking westward, and we were going to the
east. At Euphemia's request I stopped the cab,
jumped out, and ran after her, but she had disappeared in the crowd.

"She is up to mischief," said Euphemia.

But it was of no use to worry our minds on the
subject, and we soon forgot, in the ancient wonders
of the Tower, the probable eccentricities of our mod-
ern handmaid.

We returned; night came on; but Pomona was
still absent. Jonas did not know where she was, and
was very much troubled; and the baby, which had
been so skilfully kept in the background by its
mother that, so far, it had never annoyed us at all,
now began to cry, and would not be comforted. Euphemia, with the assistance of Jonas, prepared the
evening meal, and when we had nearly eaten it, Pomona came home. Euphemia asked no questions,
although she was burning with curiosity to know

where Pomona had been, considering that it was that young woman's duty to inform her without being asked.

When Pomona came in to wait on us, she acted as if she expected to be questioned, and was perfectly willing to answer, but Euphemia stood upon her dignity, and said nothing. At last Pomona could endure it no longer, and standing with a tray in her hand, she exclaimed: —

" I'm sorry I made you help git the dinner, ma'am, and I wouldn't 'a' done it for anything, but the fact is I've been to see a lord, an' was kep' late."

" What!" cried Euphemia, springing to her feet; " you don't mean that!"

And I was so amazed that I sat and looked at Pomona without saying a word.

" Yes," cried Pomona, her eyes sparkling with excitement, " I've seen a lord, and trod his floors, and I'll tell you all about it. You know I was boun' to do it, and I wanted to go alone, for if Jone was with me he'd be sure to put in some of his queer sayin's an' ten to one hurt the man's feelin's, and cut off the interview. An' as Jone said this afternoon he felt tired, with some small creeps in his back, an' didn't care to go out, I knew my time had come, and said I'd go for a walk. Day before yesterday I went up to a policeman an' I asked him if he could tell me if a lord, or a earl, or a duke lived anywhere near here. First he took me for crazy, an' then he began to ask questions which he thought was funny, but I kep' stiff to the mark, an' I made him tell me where a lord did live,

— about five blocks from here. So I fixed things all ready an' to-day I went there."

" You didn't have the assurance to suppose he'd see you ? " cried Euphemia.

" No, indeed, I hadn't," said Pomona, "at least under common circumstances. You may be sure I racked my brains enough to know what I should do to meet him face to face. It wouldn't do to go in the common way, such as ringin' at the front door and askin' for him, an' then offerin' to sell him furniter-polish for his pianner-legs. I knowed well enough that any errand like that would only bring me face to face with his bailiff, or his master of hounds, or something of that kind. So, at last, I got a plan of my own, an' I goes up the steps and rings the bell, an' when the flunkey, with more of an air of gen'ral up-liftedness about him than any one I'd seen yet, excep' Nelson on top of his pillar, opened the door an' looked at me, I asked him, —

" ' Is Earl Cobden in ? '

" At this the man opened his eyes, an' remarked : —

" ' What uv it if he is ? '

" Then I answers, firmly : —

" ' If he's in, I want yer to take him this letter, an' I'll wait here.' "

" You don't mean to say," cried Euphemia, " that you wrote the earl a letter ? "

" Yes, I did," continued Pomona, " and at first the man didn't seem inclined to take it. But I held it out so steady that he took it an' put it on a little tray, whether nickel-plated or silver I couldn't make out, and carried it up the widest and splendidest pair o' stairs that I ever see in a house jus' intended to be lived in. When he got to the fust landin' he met a gentleman, and give him the letter. When I saw this I was took aback, for I thought it was his lordship a-comin' down, an' I didn't want to have no interview with a earl at his front door. But the second glance I took at him showed me that it wasn't him. He opened it, notwithstandin', an' read it all through from beginnin' to end. When he had done it he looked down at me, and then he went back up stairs a-follered by the flunk, which last pretty soon came down ag'in an' told me I was to go up. I don't think I ever felt so much like a wringed-out dish-cloth as I did when I went up them palatial stairs. But I tried to think of things that would prop me up. P'r'aps, I thought, my ancient ancestors came to this land with his'n; who knows? An' I might 'a' been switched off on some female line, an' so lost the name an' estates. At any rate, be brave! With such thoughts as these I tried to stiffen my legs, figgeratively speakin'. We went through two or three rooms (I hadn't time to count 'em) an' then I was showed into the lofty presence of the earl. He was standin' by the fire-place, an' the minnit my eyes lit upon him I knowed it was him."

"Why, how was that?" cried Euphemia and myself almost in the same breath.

"I knowed him by his wax figger," continued Pomona, "which Jone and I see at Madame Tussaud's wax-works. They've got all the head people of these days there now, as well as the old kings and the pizeners. The clothes wasn't exactly the same, though very good on each, an' there was more of an air of shortenin' of the spine in the wax figger than in the other one. But the likeness was awful strikin'.

"'Well, my good woman,' says he, a-holdin' my open letter in his hand, 'so you want to see a lord, do you?'"

"What on earth did you write to him?" exclaimed Euphemia. "You mustn't go on a bit further until you have told what was in your letter."

"Well," said Pomona, "as near as I can remember, it was like this: '*William, Lord Cobden, Earl of Sorsetshire an' Derry. Dear Sir. Bein' brought up under Republican institutions, in the land of the free* —' I left out '*the home of the brave*' because there wasn't no use crowin' about that jus' then — '*I haven't had no oppertunity of meetin' with a individual of lordly blood. Ever since I was a small girl takin' books from the circulatin' libery, an' obliged to read out loud with divided sillerbles, I've drank in every word of the tales of lords and other nobles of high degree, that the little shops where I gen'rally got my books, an' some with the pages out at the most excitin' parts, contained. An' so I asks you now, Sir Lord* —' I did put *humbly*, but I scratched that out, bein' an American woman — '*to do me the favor of a short audience. Then, when I reads about noble earls an' dukes in their brilliant lit halls an' castles, or mounted on their champin' chargers, a-leadin' their trusty hordes to victory amid the glittering minarets of fame, I'll know what they looks like.*' An' then I signed my name.

"'Yes, sir,' says I, in answer to his earlship's question," said Pomona, taking up her story, "'I did want to see one, upon my word.'

"'An' now that you have seen him,' says he, 'what do you think of him?'

"Now, I had made up my mind before I entered this ducal pile, or put my foot on one ancestral stone, that I'd be square and honest through the whole business, and not try no counterfeit presentiments with the earl. So I says to him:—

"'The fust thing I thinks is, that you've got on the nicest suit of clothes that I've ever seed yit, not bein' exactly Sunday clothes, and yit fit for company, an' if money can buy 'em — an' men's clothes is cheap enough here, dear only knows — I'm goin' to have a suit jus' like it for Jone, my husband.' It was a kind o' brown mixed stuff, with a little spot of red in it here an' there, an' was about as gay for plain goods, an' as plain for gay goods, as anythin' could be, an' 'twas easy enough to see that it was all wool. 'Of course,' says I, 'Jone'll have his coat made different in front, for single-breasted, an' a buttonin' so high up is a'most too stylish for him, 'specially as fashions 'ud change afore the coat was wore out. But I needn't bother your earlship about that.'

"'An' so,' says he, an' I imagine I see an air of sadness steal over his features, 'it's my clothes, after all, that interest you?'

"'Oh, no,' says I, 'I mention them because they come up fust. There is, no doubt, qualities of mind and body —'

" ' Well, we won't go into that,' said his earlship, 'an' I want to ask you a question. I suppose you represent the middle class in your country ? '

" ' I don't know 'zactly where society splits with us,' says I, 'but I guess I'm somewhere nigh the crack.'

" ' Now don't you really believe,' says he, 'that you and the people of your class would be happier, an' feel safer, politically speakin', if they had among 'em a aristocracy to which they could look up to in times of trouble, as their nat'ral born gardeens ? I ask yer this because I want to know for myself what are the reel sentiments of yer people.'

" ' Well, sir,' says I, 'when your work is done, an' your kitchen cleaned up, an' your lamp lit, a lord or a duke is jus' tip-top to read about, if the type aint too fine an' the paper mean beside, which it often is in the ten-cent books; but, further than this, I must say, we aint got no use for 'em.' At that he kind o' steps back, and looks as if he was goin' to say somethin', but I puts in quick: 'But you mustn't think, my earl,' says I, 'that we undervallers you. When we remembers the field of Agincourt; and Chevy Chase; an' the Tower of London, with the block on which three lords was beheaded, with the very cuts in it which the headsman made when he chopped 'em off, as well as two crooked ones a-showin' his bad licks, which little did he think history would preserve forever; an' the old Guildhall, where down in the ancient crypt is a-hangin' our Declaration of Independence along with the Roman pots and kittles dug up in London streets; we can't forgit that if it hadn't 'a' been for your old ancestral lines as roots, we'd never been the flourishin' tree we is.'

"'Well,' said his earlship, when I'd got through, an' he kind o' looked as if he didn't know whether to laugh or not, 'if you represent the feelin's of your class in your country, I reckon they're not just ready for a aristocracy yit.'

"An' with that he give me a little nod, an' walked off into another room. It was pretty plain from this that the interview was brought to a close, an' so I come away. The flunk was all ready to show me out, an' he did it so expeditious, though quite polite, that I didn't git no chance to take a good look at the furniter and carpets, which I'd 'a' liked to have done. An' so I've talked to a real earl, an' if not in his ancestral pile, at any rate in the gorgeousest house I ever see. An' the brilliantest dream of my youth has come true."

When she had finished I rose and looked upon her.

"Pomona," said I, "we may yet visit many foreign countries. We may see kings, queens, dukes, counts, sheikhs, beys, sultans, khedives, pashas, rajahs, and I don't know what potentates besides, and I wish to say just this one thing to you. If you don't want to get yourself and us into some dreadful scrape, and perhaps bring our journeys to a sudden close, you must put a curb on your longing for communing with beings of noble blood."

"That's true, sir," said Pomona, thoughtfully, "an' I made a pretty close shave of it this time, for when I was talkin' to the earl, I was just on the p'int of tellin' him that I had such a high opinion of his kind o' folks that I once named a big black dog after one of 'em, but I jus' remembered in time, an' slipped on to somethin' else. But I trembled worse than a peanut woman with a hackman goin' round the corner to ketch a train an' his hubs just grazin' the legs of her stand. An' so I promise you, sir, that I'll put my heel on all hankerin' after potentates."

And so she made her promise. And, knowing Pomona, I felt sure that she would keep it — if she could.

# POMONA'S DAUGHTER.

IN the pretty walk, bordered by bright flowers and low, overhanging shrubbery, which lies back of the Albert Memorial, in Kensington Gardens, London, Jonas sat on a green bench, with his baby on his knee. A few nurses were pushing baby-carriages about in different parts of the walk, and there were children playing not far away. It was drawing toward the close of the afternoon, and Jonas was thinking it was nearly time to go home, when Pomona came running to him from the gorgeous monument, which she had been carefully inspecting.

"Jone," she cried, "do you know I've been lookin' at all them great men that's standin' round the bottom of the monnyment, an' though there's over a hundred of 'em, I'm sure, I can't find a American among 'em! There's poets, an' artists, an' leadin' men, scraped up from all parts, an' not one of our illustrious dead. What d'ye think of that?"

"I can't believe it," said Jonas. "If we go home with a tale like that we'll hear the recruiting-drum from Newark to Texas, and, ten to one, I'll be drafted."

"You needn't be makin' fun," said Pomona; "you

come an' see for yourself. Perhaps you kin' find jus'
one American, an' then I'll go home satisfied."

"All right," said Jonas.

And, putting the child on the bench, he told her
he'd be back in a minute, and hurried after Pomona,
to give a hasty look for the desired American.

Corinne, the offspring of Jonas and Pomona, had
some peculiarities. One of these was that she was
accustomed to stay where she was put. Ever since
she had been old enough to be carried about, she had
been carried about by one parent or the other; and,
as it was frequently necessary to set her down, she
had learned to sit and wait until she was taken up
again. She was now nearly two years old, very strong
and active, and of an intellect which had already begun to tower. She could walk very well, but Jonas
took such delight in carrying her that he seldom
appeared to recognize her ability to use her legs. She
could also talk, but how much her parents did not
know. She was a taciturn child, and preferred to
keep her thoughts to herself, and, although she sometimes astonished us all by imitating remarks she had
heard, she frequently declined to repeat the simplest
words that had been taught her.

Corinne remained on the bench about a minute
after her father had left her, and then, contrary to
her usual custom, she determined to leave the place
where she had been put. Turning over on her
stomach, after the manner of babies, she lowered her
feet to the ground. Having obtained a foothold, she
turned herself about and proceeded, with sturdy steps,

to a baby-carriage near by which had attracted her
attention. This carriage, which was unattended, contained a baby, somewhat smaller and younger than
Corinne, who sat up and gazed with youthful interest
at the visitor who stood by the side of her vehicle.
Corinne examined, with a critical eye, the carriage
and its occupant. She looked at the soft pillow at
the baby's back, and regarded with admiration the
afghan crocheted in gay colors which was spread over
its lap, and the spacious gig-top which shielded it
from the sun. She stooped down and looked at the
wheels, and stood up and gazed at the blue eyes and
canary hair of the little occupant. Then, in quiet but
decided tones, Corinne said: —

"Dit out!"

The other baby looked at her, but made no movement to obey. After waiting a few moments, an expression of stern severity spreading itself the while
over her countenance, Corinne reached over and put
her arms around the fair-haired child. Then, with
all her weight and strength, she threw herself backward and downward. The other baby, being light,
was thus drawn bodily out of its carriage, and Corinne
sat heavily upon the ground, her new acquaintance
sprawling in her lap. Notwithstanding that she bore
the brunt of the fall upon the gravel, Corinne uttered
no cry; but, disengaging herself from her encumbrance, she rose to her feet. The other baby imitated
her, and Corinne, taking her by the hand, led her to
the bench where she herself had been left.

"Dit up!" said Corinne.

This, however, the other baby was unable to do ;
but she stood quite still, evidently greatly interested
in the proceedings.  Corinne left her and walked to
the little carriage, into which she proceeded to climb.
After some extraordinary exertions, during which her
fat legs were frequently thrust through the spokes of
the wheels and ruthlessly drawn out again, she tumbled in.  Arranging herself as comfortably as she
knew how, she drew the gay afghan over her, leaned
back upon the soft pillow, gazed up at the sheltering
gig-top, and resigned herself to luxurious bliss.  At
this supreme moment, the nurse who had had ᴄharge
of the carriage and its occupant came hurrying around
a corner of the path.  She had been taking leave of
some of her nurse-maid friends, and had stayed longer
than she had intended.  It was necessary for her to
take a suitable leave of these ladies, for that night
she was going on a journey.  She had been told to
take the baby out for an airing, and to bring it back
early.  Now, to her surprise, the afternoon had nearly
gone, and hurrying to the little carriage she seized the
handle at the back and rapidly pushed it home, without stopping to look beneath the overhanging gig-top,
or at the green bench, with which her somewhat
worried soul had no concern.  If anything could add
to Corinne's ecstatic delight, it was this charming
motion.  Closing her eyes contentedly, she dropped
asleep.

The baby with canary hair looked at the receding
nurse and carriage with widening eyes and reddening
cheeks.  Then, opening her mouth, she uttered the

cry of the deserted; but the panic-stricken nurse did not hear her, and, if she had, what were the cries of other children to her? Her only business was to get home quickly with her young charge.

About five minutes after these events, Jonas and Pomona came hurrying along the path. They, too, had stayed away much longer than they had intended, and had suddenly given up their search for the American, whom they had hoped to find in high relief upon the base of the Albert Memorial. Stepping quickly to the child, who still stood sobbing by the bench, Jonas exclaimed, "You poor itty —— !"

And then he stopped suddenly. Pomona also stood for a second, and then she made a dash at the child, and snatched it up. Gazing sharply at its tear-smeared countenance, she exclaimed, "What's this?"

The baby did not seem able to explain what it was, and only answered by a tearful sob. Jonas did not say a word; but, with the lithe quickness of a dog after a rat, he began to search behind and under benches, in the bushes, on the grass, here, there, and everywhere.

About nine o'clock that evening, Pomona came to us with tears in her eyes, and the canary-haired baby in her arms, and told us that Corinne was lost. They had searched everywhere; they had gone to the police; telegrams had been sent to every station; they had done everything that could be done, but had found no trace of the child.

"If I hadn't this," sobbed Pomona, holding out the child, "I believe I'd go wild. It isn't that she can

take the place of my dear baby, but by a-keepin' hold
of her I believe we'll git on the track of Corinne."

We were both much affected by this news, and
Euphemia joined Pomona in her tears.

"Jonas is scourin' the town yet," said Pomona.
"He'll never give up till he drops. But I felt you
ought to know, and I couldn't keep this little thing
in the night-air no longer. It's a sweet child, and its
clothes are lovely. If it's got a mother, she's bound
to want to see it before long; an' if ever I ketch sight
of her, she don't git away from me till I have my
child."

"It is a very extraordinary case," I said. "Children are often stolen, but it is seldom we hear of one
being taken and another left in its place, especially
when the children are of different ages, and totally
unlike."

"That's so," said Pomona. "At first, I thought
that Corinne had been changed off for a princess, or
something like that, but nobody couldn't make anybody believe that my big, black-haired baby was this
white-an'-yaller thing."

"Can't you find any mark on her clothes," asked
Euphemia, "by which you could discover her parentage? If there are no initials, perhaps you can find a
coronet or a coat of arms."

"No," said Pomona, "there aint nothin'. I've
looked careful. But there's great comfort to think
that Corinne's well stamped."

"Stamped!" we exclaimed. "What do you mean
by that?"

"Why, you see," answered Pomona, "when Jone an' I was goin' to bring our baby over here among so many million people, we thought there might be danger of its gittin' lost or mislaid, though we never really believed any such thing would happen, or we wouldn't have come. An' so we agreed to mark her, for I've often read about babies bein' stole an' kept two or three years, and when found bein' so changed their own mothers didn't know 'em. Jone said we'd better tattoo Corinne, for them marks would always be there, but I wouldn't agree to have the little creature's skin stuck with needles, not even after Jone said we might give her chloryform; so we agreed to stamp initials on her with Perkins's Indelible Dab. It is intended to mark sheep, but it don't hurt, and it don't never come off. We put the letters on the back of her heels, where they wouldn't show, for she's never to go barefoot, an' where they'd be easy got at if we wanted to find 'em. We put R. G. on one heel for the name of the place, and J. P. on the other heel for Jonas an' me. If, twenty years from now," said Pomona, her tears welling out afresh, "I should see a young woman with eyes like Corinne's, an' that I felt was her, a-walking up to the bridal altar, with all the white flowers, an' the floatin' veils, an' the crowds in the church, an' the music playin', an' the minister all ready, I'd jist jerk that young woman into the vestry-room, an' have off her shoes an' stockin's in no time. An' if she had R. G. on one heel, an' J. P. on the other, that bridegroom could go home alone."

We confidently assured Pomona that with such

means of identification, and the united action of ourselves and the police, the child would surely be found,
and we accompanied her to her lodgings, which were
now in a house not far from our own.

When the nurse reached home with the little carriage it was almost dark, and, snatching up the child,
she ran to the nursery without meeting any one.
The child felt heavy, but she was in such a hurry she
scarcely noticed that. She put it upon the bed, and
then lighting the gas she unwrapped the afghan, in
which the little creature was now almost entirely en-
veloped. When she saw the face, and the black hair,
from which the cap had fallen off, she was nearly
frightened to death, but, fortunately for herself, she
did not scream. She was rather a stupid woman, with
but few ideas, but she could not fail to see that some
one had taken her charge, and put this child in its
place. Her first impulse was to run back to the gardens, but she felt certain that her baby had been
carried off; and, besides, she could not, without dis-
covery, leave the child here or take it with her; and
while she stood in dumb horror, her mistress sent for
her. The lady was just going out to dinner, and told
the nurse that, as they were all to start for the Continent by the tidal train, which left at ten o'clock that
night, she must be ready with the baby, well wrapped
up for the journey. The half-stupefied woman had no
words nor courage with which to declare, at this moment, the true state of the case. She said nothing,
and went back to the nursery and sat there in dumb
consternation, and without sense enough to make a

plan of any kind. The strange child soon awoke and began to cry, and then the nurse mechanically fed it, and it went to sleep again. When the summons came to her to prepare for the journey, in cowardly haste she wrapped the baby, so carefully covering its head that she scarcely gave it a chance to breathe; and she and the lady's waiting-maid were sent in a cab to the Victoria Station. The lady was travelling with a party of friends, and the nurse and the waiting-maid were placed in the adjoining compartment of the railway-carriage. On the six hours' channel passage from Newhaven to Dieppe the lady was extremely sick, and reached France in such a condition that she had to be almost carried on shore. It had been her intention to stop a few days at this fashionable watering-place, but she declared that she must go straight on to Paris, where she could be properly attended to, and, moreover, that she never wanted to see the sea again. When she had been placed in the train for Paris she sent for the nurse, and feebly asked how the baby was, and if it had been seasick. On being told that it was all right, and had not shown a sign of illness, she expressed her gratification, and lay back among her rugs.

The nurse and the waiting-maid travelled together, as before, but the latter, wearied by her night's attendance upon her mistress, slept all the way from Dieppe to Paris. When they reached that city, they went into the waiting-room until a carriage could be procured for them, and there the nurse, placing the baby on a seat, asked her companion to take care of it for a few minutes. She then went out of the station door, and disappeared into Paris.

In this way, the brunt of the terrible disclosure, which came very soon, was thrown upon the waiting-maid. No one, however, attached any blame to her: of course, the absconding nurse had carried away the fair-haired child. The waiting-maid had been separated from her during the passage from the train to the station, and it was supposed that in this way an exchange of babies had been easily made by her and her confederates. When the mother knew of her loss, her grief was so violent that for a time her life was in danger. All Paris was searched by the police and her friends, but no traces could be found of the wicked nurse and the fair-haired child. Money, which, of course, was considered the object of the inhuman crime, was freely offered, but to no avail. No one imagined for an instant that the exchange was made before the party reached Paris. It seemed plain enough that the crime was committed when the woman fled.

Corinne, who had been placed in the charge of a servant until it was determined what to do with her, was not at all satisfied with the new state of affairs, and loudly demanded her papa and mamma, behaving for a time in a very turbulent way. In a few days, the lady recovered her strength, and asked to see this child. The initials upon Corinne's heels had been discovered, and, when she was told of these, the lady examined them closely.

"The people who left this child," she exclaimed,

"do not intend to lose her! They know where she is, and they will keep a watch upon her, and when they get a chance they will take her. I, too, will keep a watch upon her, and when they come for her I shall see them."

Her use of words soon showed Corinne to be of English parentage, and it was generally supposed that she had been stolen from some travellers, and had been used at the station as a means of giving time to the nurse to get away with the other child.

In accord with her resolution, the grief-stricken lady put Corinne in the charge of a trusty woman, and, moreover, scarcely ever allowed her to be out of her sight.

It was suggested that advertisement be made for the parents of a child marked with R. G. and J. P. But to this the lady decidedly objected.

"If her parents find her," she said, "they will take her away; and I want to keep her till the thieves come for her. I have lost my child, and as this one is the only clue I shall ever have to her, I intend to keep it. When I have found my child, it will be time enough to restore this one."

Thus selfish is maternal love.

Pomona bore up better under the loss than did Jonas. Neither of them gave up the search for a day; but Jonas, haggard and worn, wandered aimlessly about the city, visiting every place into which he imagined a child might have wandered, or might have been taken, searching even to the crypt in the Guildhall and the Tower of London. Pomona's mind worked quite as actively as her husband's body. She took great care of "Little Kensington," as she called the strange child from the place where she had been found; and therefore could not go about as Jonas did. After days and nights of ceaseless supposition, she had come to the conclusion that Corinne had been stolen by opera singers.

"I suppose you never knew it," she said to us, "for I took pains not to let it disturb you, but that child has notes in her voice about two stories higher than any operer prymer donner that I ever heard, an' I've heard lots of 'em, for I used to go into the top gallery of the operer as often as into the theayter; an' if any operer singer ever heard them high notes of Corinne's, — an' there was times when she'd let 'em out without the least bit of a notice, — it's them that's took her."

"But, my poor Pomona," said Euphemia, "you don't suppose that little child could be of any use to an opera singer; at least, not for years and years."

"Oh, yes, ma'am," replied Pomona; "she was none too little. Sopranners is like mocking-birds; they've got to be took young."

No arguments could shake Pomona's belief in this theory. And she daily lamented the fact that there was no opera in London at that time that she might go to the performances, and see if there was any one on the stage who looked mean enough to steal a child.

"If she was there," said Pomona, "I'd know it. She'd feel the scorn of a mother's eye on her, an' her guilty heart would make her forget her part."

Pomona frequently went into Kensington Gardens, and laid traps for opera singers who might be sojourning in London. She would take Little Kensington into the gardens, and, placing her carefully in the corner of a bench, would retire to a short distance and pretend to be absorbed in a book, while her sharp eyes kept up the watch for a long-haired tenor, or a beautifully dressed soprano, who should suddenly rush out from the bushes and seize the child.

" I wouldn't make no fuss if they was to come out," she said. "Little Kensington would go under my arm, not theirn, an' I'd walk calmly with 'em to their home. Then I'd say : ' Give me my child, an' take yourn, which, though she probably hasn't got no voice, is a lot too good for you; and may the house hurl stools at you the next time you appear, is the limit of a mother's curse.' "

But, alas for Pomona, no opera singers ever showed themselves.

These days of our stay in London were not pleasant. We went about little, and enjoyed nothing. At last Pomona came to us, her face pale but determined.

" It's no use," she said, "for us to keep you here no longer, when I know you've got through with the place, and want to go on, an' we'll go, too, for I don't believe my child's in London. She's been took away, an' we might as well look for her in one place as another. The perlice tells us that if she's found here, they'll know it fust, an' they'll telegraph to us wherever we is; an' if it wasn't fur nuthin' else, it would be a mercy to git Jone out of this place. He goes about

like a cat after her drowned kittens. It's a-bringin'
out them chills of hisn, an' the next thing it'll kill
him. I can't make him believe in the findin' of Corinne as firm as I do, but I know as long as Perkins's
Indelible Dab holds out (an' there's no rubbin' nor
washin' it off) I'll git my child."

I admitted, but not with Pomona's hopefulness,
that the child might be found as easily in Paris as here.

"And we've seen everything about London," said
Euphemia, "except Windsor Castle. I did want, and
still want, to see just how the Queen keeps house, and
perhaps get some ideas which might be useful; but
Her Majesty is away now, and, although they say
that's the time to go there, it is not the time for me.
You'll not find me going about inspecting domestic
arrangements when the lady of the house is away."

So we packed up and went to Paris, taking Little
Kensington along. Notwithstanding our great sympathy with Corinne's parents, Euphemia and myself
could not help becoming somewhat resigned to the
affliction which had befallen them, and we found ourselves obliged to enjoy the trip very much. Euphemia
became greatly excited and exhilarated as we entered
Paris. For weeks I knew she had been pining for
this city. As she stepped from the train she seemed
to breathe a new air, and her eyes sparkled as she
knew by the prattle and cries about her that she was
really in France.

We were obliged to wait some time in the station
before we could claim our baggage, and while we were
standing there Euphemia drew my attention to a

placard on the wall. " Look at that ! " she exclaimed.
" Even here, on our very entrance to the city, we see
signs of that politeness which is the very heart of the
nation. I can't read the whole of that notice from
here, but those words in large letters show that it
refers to the observance of the ancient etiquettes.
Think of it ! Here in a railroad station people are
expected to behave to each other with the old-time
dignity and gallantry of our forefathers. I tell you
it thrills my very soul to think I am among such a
people, and I am glad they can't understand what I
say, so that I may speak right out."

I never had the heart to throw cold water on Euphemia's noble emotions, and so I did not tell her that
the notice merely requested travellers to remove from
their trunks the *anciennes étiquettes,* or old railway
labels.

We were not rich tourists, and we all took lodgings
in a small hotel to which we had been recommended.
It was in the Latin Quarter, near the river, and opposite the vast palace of the Louvre, into whose laby-
rinth of picture-galleries Euphemia and I were eager
to plunge.

But first we all went to the office of the American
Consul, and consulted him in regard to the proper
measures to be taken for searching for the little
Corinne in Paris. After that, for some days, Jonas
and Pomona spent all their time, and Euphemia and I
part of ours, in looking for the child. Euphemia's
Parisian exhilaration continued to increase, but there
were some things that disappointed her.

"I thought," said she, "that people in France took their morning coffee in bed, but they do not bring it up to us."

"But, my dear," said I, "I am sure you said before we came here that you considered taking coffee in bed as an abominable habit, and that nothing could ever make you like it."

"I know," said she, "that I have always thought it a lazy custom, and not a bit nice, and I think so yet. But still, when we are in a strange country, I expect to live as other people do."

It was quite evident that Euphemia had been looking forward for some time to the novel experience of taking her coffee in bed. But the gray-haired old gentleman who acted as our chambermaid never hinted that he supposed we wanted anything of the kind.

Nothing, however, excited Euphemia's indignation so much as the practice of giving a *pourboire* to cabmen and others. "It is simply feeding the flames of intemperance," she said. When she had occasion to take a cab by herself, she never conformed to this reprehensible custom. When she paid the driver, she would add something to the regular fare, but as she gave it to him she would say in her most distinct French: "*Pour manger. Comprenezvous?*" The *cocher* would generally nod his head, and thank her very kindly, which he had good reason to do, for she never forgot that it took more money to buy food than drink.

In spite of the attractions of the city, our sojourn

in Paris was not satisfactory. Apart from the family
trouble which oppressed us, it rained nearly all the
time. We were told that in order to see Paris at its
best we should come in the spring. In the month of
May it was charming. Then everybody would be out-
of-doors, and we would see a whole city enjoying life.
As we wished to enjoy life without waiting for the
spring, we determined to move southward, and visit
during the winter those parts of Europe which then
lay under blue skies and a warm sun. It was impossible, at present, for Pomona and Jonas to enjoy life
anywhere, and they would remain in Paris, and then,
if they did not find their child in a reasonable time,
they would join us. Neither of them understood
French, but this did not trouble them in the slightest.
Early in their Paris wanderings they had met with a
boy who had once lived in New York, and they had
taken him into pay as an interpreter. He charged
them a franc and a half a day, and I am sure they got
their money's worth.

Soon after we had made up our minds to move
toward the south, I came home from a visit to the
bankers, and joyfully told Euphemia that I had met
Baxter.

"Baxter?" said she, inquiringly; "who is he?"

"I used to go to school with him," I said; "and to
think that I should meet him here!"

"I never heard you mention him before," she remarked.

"No," I answered; "it must be fifteen or sixteen
years since I have seen him, and really it is a great

pleasure to meet him here. He is a capital fellow. He was very glad to see me."

"I should think," said Euphemia, "if you like each other so much that you would have exchanged visits in America, or, at least, have corresponded."

"Oh, it is a very different thing at home," I said; "but here it is delightful to meet an old school friend like Baxter. He is coming to see us this evening."

That evening Baxter came. He was delighted to meet Euphemia, and inquired with much solicitude about our plans and movements. He had never heard of my marriage, and, for years, had not known whether I was dead or alive. Now he took the keenest interest in me and mine. We were a little sorry to find that this was not Baxter's first visit to Europe. He had been here several times; and, as he expressed it, "had knocked about a good deal over the Continent." He was dreadfully familiar with everything, and talked about some places we were longing to see in a way that considerably dampened our enthusiasm. In fact, there was about him an air of superiority which, though tempered by much kindliness, was not altogether agreeable. He highly approved our idea of leaving Paris. "The city is nothing now," he said. "You ought to see it in May." We said we had heard that, and then spoke of Italy. "You mustn't go there in the winter," he said. "You don't see the country at its best. May is the time for Italy. Then it is neither too hot nor too cold, and you will find out what an Italian sky is." We said that we hoped to be in England in the spring, and he agreed that we were right there. "England is never so lovely as in May." .

"Well!" exclaimed Euphemia; "it seems to me, from all I hear, that we ought to take about twelve years to see Europe. We should leave the United States every April, spend May in some one place, and go back in June. And this we ought to do each year until we have seen all the places in May. This might do very well for any one who had plenty of money, and who liked the ocean, but I don't think we could stand it. As for me," she continued, "I would like to spend these months, so cold and disagreeable here, in the sunny lands of Southern France. I want to see the vineyards and the olive groves, and the dark-eyed maidens singing in the fields. I long for the soft skies of Provence, and to hear the musical dialect in which Frederic Mistral wrote his ' Miréio.' "

"That sounds very well," said Baxter, " but in all those southern countries you must be prepared in winter for the rigors of the climate. The sun is pretty warm sometimes at this season, but as soon as you get out of it you will freeze to death if you are not careful. The only way to keep warm is to be in the sun, out of the wind, and that won't work on rainy days, and winter is the rainy season, you know. In the houses it is as cold as ice, and the fires don't amount to any-thing. You might as well light a bundle of wooden tooth-picks and put it in the fire-place. If you could sleep all the time you might be comfortable, for they give you a feather-bed to cover yourself with. Out-side you may do well enough if you keep up a steady walking, but indoors you will have hard work to keep warm. You must wear chest-protectors. They sell them down there — great big ones, made of rabbit-skins; and a nice thing for a man to have to wear in the house is a pair of cloth bags lined with fur. They would keep his feet and legs warm when he isn't walking. It is well, too, to have a pair of smaller fur bags for your hands when you are in the house. You can have a little hole in the end of one of them through which you can stick a pen-holder, and then you can write letters. An india-rubber bag, filled with hot water, to lower down your back, is a great comfort. You haven't any idea how cold your spine gets in those warm countries. And, if I were you, I'd avoid a place where you see them carting coal stoves around. Those are the worst spots. And you need not expect to get one of the stoves, not while they can sell you wood at two sticks for a franc. You had better go to some place where they are not accustomed to having tourists. In the regular resorts they are afraid to make any show of keeping warm, for fear people will think they are in the habit of having cold weather. And in Italy you've got to be precious careful, or you'll be taken sick. And another thing. I suppose you brought a great deal of baggage with you. You, for instance," said our friend, turning to me, "packed up, I suppose, a heavy over-coat for cold weather, and a lighter one, and a good winter suit, and a good summer one, besides another for spring and fall, and an old suit to lie about in in the orange groves, and a dress suit, besides such convenient articles as old boots for tramping in, pocket-lanterns, and so forth."

Strange to say, I had all these, besides many other things of a similar kind, and I could not help admitting it.

"Well," said Baxter, "you'd better get rid of the most of that as soon as you can, for if you travel with that sort of heavy weight in the Mediterranean countries, you might as well write home and get your house mortgaged. All along the lines of travel, in the south of Europe, you find the hotels piled up with American baggage left there by travellers, who'll never send for it. It reminds one of the rows of ox skeletons that used to mark out the roads to California. But I guess you'll be able to stick it out. Good bye. Let me hear from you."

When Baxter left us, we could not but feel a little down-hearted, and Euphemia turned to her guide-book to see if his remarks were corroborated there.

"Well, there is one comfort," she exclaimed at last; "this book says that in Naples epidemias are not so deadly as they are in some other places, and if the traveller observes about a page of directions, which are given here, and consults a physician the moment he feels himself out of order, it is quite possible to ward off attacks of fever. That is encouraging, and I think we might as well go on."

"Yes," said I, "and here, in this newspaper, a hotel in Venice advertises that its situation enables it to avoid the odors of the Grand Canal; and an undertaker in Nice advertises that he will forward the

corpses of tourists to all parts of Europe and America.
I think there is a chance of our getting back, either
dead or alive, and so I also say, let us go on."

But before we left Paris, we determined to go to
the Grand Opera, which we had not yet visited, and
Euphemia proposed that we should take Pomona with
us. The poor girl was looking wretched and woe-
begone, and needed to have her mind diverted from
her trouble. Jonas, at the best of times, could not be
persuaded to any amusement of this sort, but Pomona
agreed to go. We had no idea of dressing for the
boxes, and we took good front seats in the upper
circle, where we could see the whole interior of the
splendid house. As soon as the performance com-
menced, the old dramatic fire began to burn in Pomona. Her eyes sparkled as they had not done for
many a day, and she really looked like her own bright
self. The opera was "Le Prophète," and, as none of
us had ever seen anything produced on so magnificent
a scale, we were greatly interested, especially in the
act which opens with that wonderful winter scene in
the forest, with hundreds of people scattered about
under the great trees, with horses and sleighs and
the frozen river in the background where the skaters
came gliding on. The grouping was picturesque and
artistic; the scale of the scene was immense; there
was a vast concourse of people on the stage; the
dances were beautiful; the merry skaters graceful;
the music was inspiring.

Suddenly, above the voices of the chorus, above the
drums and bass strings of the orchestra, above the

highest notes of the sopranos, above the great chande-
lier itself, came two notes distinct and plain, and the
words to which they were set, were : —

"Ma-ma!"

Like a shot Pomona was on her feet. With arms
outspread and her whole figure dilating until she
seemed twice as large as usual, I thought she was
about to spring over the balcony into the house below.
I clutched her, and Euphemia and I, both upon our feet,
followed her gaze and saw upon the stage a little girl in
gay array, and upturned face. It was the lost Corinne.

Without a word, Pomona made a sudden turn,
sprang up the steps behind her, and out upon the
lobby, Euphemia and I close behind her. Around
and down the steps we swept, from lobby to lobby,
amazing the cloak-keepers and attendants, but stopping for nothing; down the grand staircase like an
avalanche, almost into the arms of the astonished
military sentinels, who, startled from their soldier-
like propriety, sprang, muskets in hand, toward us.
It was only then that I was able to speak to Pomona,
and breathlessly ask her where she was going.

"To the stage-door!" she cried, making a motion
to hurl to the ground the soldier before her. But
there was no need to go to any stage-door. In a
moment there rushed along the corridor a lady, dressed
apparently in all the colors of the rainbow, and bear-
ing in her arms a child. There was a quick swoop,
and in another moment Pomona had the child. But
clinging to its garments, the lady cried, in excellent
English, but with some foreign tinge : —

"Where is my child you stole ? "

"Stole your grandmother!" briefly ejaculated Pomona. And then, in grand forgetfulness of everything but her great joy, she folded her arms around
her child, and standing like a statue of motherly content, she seemed, in our eyes, to rise to the regions of
the caryatides and the ceiling frescos. Not another
word she spoke, and amid the confusion of questions
and exclamations, and the wild demands of the lady,
Euphemia and I contrived to make her understand
the true state of the case, and that her child was
probably at our lodgings. Then there were great exclamations and quick commands; and, directly, four
of us were in a carriage whirling to our hotel. All
the way, Pomona sat silent with her child clasped
tightly, while Euphemia and I kept up an earnest but
unsatisfactory conversation with the lady; for, as to
this strange affair, we could tell each other but little.
We learned from the lady, who was an assistant
soprano at the Grand Opera, how Corinne came to her
in Paris, and how she had always kept her with her,
even dressing her up, and taking her on the stage in
that great act where as many men, women, and children as possible were brought upon the scene. When
she heard the cry of Corinne, she knew the child had
seen its mother, and then, whether the opera went on
or not, it mattered not to her.

When the carriage stopped, the three women sprang
out at once, and how they all got through the door,
I cannot tell. There was such a tremendous ring at
the gate of the court that the old *concierge*, who

opened it by pulling a wire in his little den somewhere in the rear, must have been dreadfully startled
in his sleep. We rushed through the court and up
the stairs past our apartments to Pomona's room; and
there in the open doorway stood Jonas, his coat off,
his sandy hair in wild confusion, his face radiant, and
in his hands Little Kensington in her nightgown.

"I knew by the row on the stairs you'd brought
her home," he exclaimed, as Little Kensington was
snatched from him and Corinne was put into his arms.

We left Jonas and Pomona to their wild delight,
and I accompanied the equally happy lady to the
opera house, where I took occasion to reclaim the
wraps which we had left behind in our sudden flight.

When the police of Paris were told to give up their
search for an absconding nurse accompanied by a child,
and to look for one without such encumbrance, they
found her. From this woman was obtained much of
the story I have told, and a good deal more was drawn
out, little by little, from Corinne, who took especial
pleasure in telling, in brief sentences, how she had
ousted the lazy baby from the carriage, and how she
had scratched her own legs in getting in.

"What I'm proud of," said Pomona, "is that she
did it all herself. It wasn't none of your common
stealin's an' findin's; an' it aint everywhere you'll see
a child that kin git itself lost back of Prince Albert's
monnyment, an' git itself found at the operer in Paris,
an' attend to both ends of the case itself. An', after
all, them two high notes of hern was more good than
Perkins's Indelible Dab."

# DERELICT.

A TALE OF THE WAYWARD SEA.

## I.

ON the 25th of May, 1887, I sat alone upon the deck of the *Sparhawk*, a three-masted schooner, built, according to a description in the cabin, at Sackport, Me. I was not only alone on the deck, but I was alone on the ship. The *Sparhawk* was a "derelict"; that is, if a vessel with a man on board of her can be said to be totally abandoned.

I had now been on board the schooner for eight days. How long before that she had been drifting about at the mercy of the winds and currents I did not then know, but I discovered afterward that during a cyclone early in April she had been abandoned by her entire crew, and had since been reported five times to the hydrographic office of the Navy Department in Washington, and her positions and probable courses duly marked on the pilot chart.

She had now become one of that little fleet abandoned at sea for one cause or another, and floating about this way and that, as the wild winds blew or the ocean currents ran. Voyaging without purpose, as if manned by the spirits of ignorant landsmen, sometimes backward and forward over comparatively

78

small ocean spaces, and sometimes drifting for many months and over thousands of miles, these derelicts form, at night and in fog, one of the dangers most to be feared by those who sail upon the sea.

As I said before, I came on board the abandoned *Sparhawk* on the 17th of May, and very glad indeed was I to get my feet again on solid planking. Three days previously the small steamer *Thespia*, from Havana to New York, on which I had been a passenger, had been burned at sea, and all on board had left her in the boats.

What became of the other boats I do not know, but the one in which I found myself in company with five other men, all Cuban cigarmakers, was nearly upset by a heavy wave during the second night we were out, and we were all thrown into the sea. As none of the Cubans could swim, they were all lost, but I succeeded in reaching the boat, which had righted itself, though half full of water.

There was nothing in the boat but two oars which had not slipped out of their rowlocks, a leather scoop which had been tied to a thwart, and the aforementioned water.

Before morning I had nearly baled out the boat, and fortunate it was for me that up to the time of the upset we had had enough to eat and drink, for otherwise I should not have had strength for that work and for what followed.

Not long after daybreak I sighted the *Sparhawk*, and immediately began to make such signals as I could. The vessel appeared to be but a few miles distant, and I could not determine whether she was approaching me or going away from me. I could see no sign that my signals had been noticed, and began frantically to row toward her. After a quarter of an hour of violent exertion, I did not appear to be much nearer to her; but, observing her more closely, I could see, even with my landsman's eyes, that something was the matter with her. Portions of her mast and rigging were gone, and one large sail at her stern appeared to be fluttering in the wind.

But it mattered not to me what had happened to her. She was a ship afloat, and I must reach her. Tired, hungry, and thirsty I rowed and rowed, but it was not until long after noon that I reached her. She must have been much farther from me than I had supposed.

With a great deal of trouble I managed to clamber on board, and found the ship deserted. I had suspected that this would be the case, for as I had drawn near I would have seen some sign that my approach was noticed had there been anybody on board to perceive it. But I found food and water, and when I was no longer hungry or thirsty I threw myself in a berth, and slept until the sun was high the next day.

I had now been on the derelict vessel for eight days. Why she had been deserted and left to her fate I was not seaman enough to know. It is true that her masts and rigging were in a doleful condition, but she did not appear to be leaking, and rode well upon the sea. There was plenty of food and water on board, and comfortable accommodations. I afterwards learned that during the terrible cyclone which had overtaken her, she had been on her beam ends for an hour before the crew left her in the boats.

For the first day or two of my sojourn on the *Sparhawk* I was as happy as a man could be under the circumstances. I thought myself to be perfectly safe, and believed it could not be long before I would be picked up. Of course I did not know my latitude and longitude, but I felt sure that the part of the Atlantic in which I was must be frequently crossed by steamers and other vessels.

About the fourth day I began to feel uneasy. I had seen but three sails, and these had taken no notice of the signal which I had hung as high in the mizzen-mast as I had dared to climb. It was, indeed, no wonder that the signal had attracted no attention among the fluttering shreds of sails about it.

I believe that one ship must have approached quite near me. I had been below some time, looking over the books in the captain's room, and when I came on deck I saw the stern of the ship, perhaps a mile or two distant, and sailing away. Of course my shouts and wavings were of no avail. She had probably recognized the derelict *Sparhawk* and had made a note of her present position, in order to report to the hydrographic office.

The weather had been fair for the most part of the time, the sea moderately smooth, and when the wind was strong, the great sail on the mizzen-mast, which remained hoisted and which I had tightened up a little, acted after the manner of the long end of a weather-vane, and kept the ship's head to the sea.

Thus it will be seen that I was not in a bad plight; but although I appreciated this, I grew more and more troubled and uneasy. For several days I had not seen a sail, and if I should see one how could I attract attention? It must be that the condition of the vessel indicated that there was no one on board. Had I known that the *Sparhawk* was already entered upon the list of derelicts, I should have been hopeless indeed.

At first I hung out a lantern as a night signal, but on the second night it was broken by the wind, and I could find only one other in good condition. The ship's lights must have been blown away in the storm, together with her boats and much of her rigging. I would not hang out the only lantern left me, for fear it should come to grief, and that I should be left in the dark at night in that great vessel. Had I known that I was on a vessel which had been regularly relegated to the ranks of the forsaken, I should better have appreciated the importance of allowing passing vessels to see that there was a light on board the *Sparhawk*, and, therefore, in all probability a life.

As day after day had passed, I had become more and more disheartened. It seemed to me that I was in a part of the great ocean avoided by vessels of every kind, that I was not in the track of anything going anywhere. Every day there seemed to be less and less wind, and when I had been on board a week, the *Sparhawk* was gently rising and falling on a

smooth sea in a dead calm. Hour after hour I swept
the horizon with the captain's glass, but only once did
I see anything to encourage me. This was what appeared like a long line of black smoke against the distant sky, which might have been left by a passing
steamer; but, were this the case, I never saw the
steamer.

Happily, there were plenty of provisions on board
of a plain kind. I found spirits and wine, and even
medicines, and in the captain's room there were pipes,
tobacco, and some books.

This comparative comfort gave me a new and
strange kind of despair. I began to fear that I might
become contented to live out my life alone in the
midst of this lonely ocean. In that case, what sort of
a man should I become?

It was about 8.30 by the captain's chronometer,
when I came on deck on the morning of the 25th of
May. I had become a late riser, for what was the
good of rising early when there was nothing to rise
for? I had scarcely raised my eyes above the rail of
the ship when, to my utter amazement, I perceived a
vessel not a mile away. The sight was so unexpected,
and the surprise was so great, that my heart almost
stopped beating as I stood and gazed at her.

She was a medium-sized iron steamer, and lay upon
the sea in a peculiar fashion, her head being much
lower than her stern, the latter elevated so much that
I could see part of the blades of her motionless pro-
peller. She presented the appearance of a ship which
was just about to plunge, bow foremost, into the

depths of the ocean, or which had just risen, stern
foremost, from those depths.

With the exception of her position, and the fact
that no smoke-stack was visible, she seemed, to my
eyes, to be in good enough trim. She had probably
been in collision with something, and her forward
compartments had filled. Deserted by her crew, she
had become a derelict, and, drifting about in her deso-
lation, had fallen in with another derelict as desolate
as herself. The fact that I was on board the *Sparhawk* did not, in my eyes, make that vessel any the
less forsaken and forlorn.

The coming of this steamer gave me no comfort.
Two derelicts, in their saddening effects upon the
spirits, would be twice as bad as one, and, more than
that, there was danger, should a storm arise, that they
would dash into each other and both go to the bottom.
Despairing as I had become, I did not want to go to
the bottom.

As I gazed upon the steamer I could see that she
was gradually approaching me. There was a little
breeze this morning, and so much of her hull stood
out of the water that it caught a good deal of the
wind. The *Sparhawk*, on the contrary, was but little
affected by the breeze, for apart from the fact that the
great sail kept her head always to the wind, she was
heavily laden with sugar and molasses and sat deep in
the water. The other was not coming directly toward
me, but would probably pass at a considerable distance. I did not at all desire that she should come
near the *Sparhawk*.

Suddenly my heart gave a jump. I could distinctly see on the stern of the steamer the flutter of something white. It was waved! Somebody must be waving it!

Hitherto I had not thought of the spyglass, for with my naked eyes I could see all that I cared to see of the vessel, but now I dashed below to get it. When I brought it to bear upon the steamer I saw plainly that the white object was waved by some one, and that some one was a woman. I could see above the rail the upper part of her body, her uncovered head, her uplifted arm wildly waving.

Presently the waving ceased, and then the thought suddenly struck me that, receiving no response, she had in despair given up signalling. Cursing my stupidity, I jerked my handkerchief from my pocket, and, climbing a little way into the rigging, I began to wave it madly. Almost instantly her waving recommenced. I soon stopped signalling, and so did she. No more of that was needed. I sprang to the deck and took up the glass.

The woman was gone, but in a few moments she reappeared armed with a glass. This action filled me with amazement. Could it be possible that the woman was alone on the steamer, and that there was no one else to signal and to look out? The thing was incredible, and yet, if there were men on board, why did they not show themselves? And why did not one of them wave the signal and use the glass?

The steamer was steadily but very slowly nearing the *Sparhawk*, when the woman removed the glass and stood up waist high above the rail of the steamer.

Now I could see her much better; I fancied I could almost discern her features. She was not old; she was well shaped; her bluish gray dress fitted her snugly. Holding the rail with one hand she stood up very erect, which must have been somewhat difficult, considering the inclination of the deck. For a moment I fancied I had seen or known some one whose habit it was to stand up very erect as this woman stood upon the steamer. The notion was banished as absurd.

Wondering what I should do, what instant action I should take, I laid down my glass, and as I did so the woman immediately put up hers. Her object was plain enough; she wanted to observe me, which she could not well do when a view of my face was obstructed by the glass and my outstretched arms. I was sorry that I had not sooner given her that opportunity, and for some moments I stood and faced her, waving my hat as I did so.

I was wild with excitement. What should I do? What could I do? There were no boats on the *Sparhawk,* and what had become of the one in which I reached her I did not know. Thinking of nothing but getting on board the vessel, I had forgotten to make the boat fast, and when I went to look for it a day or two afterward it was gone. On the steamer, however, I saw a boat hanging from davits near the stern. There was hope in that.

But there might be no need for a boat. Under the influence of the gentle breeze, the steamer was steadily drawing nearer to the *Sparhawk.* Perhaps they might touch each other. But this idea was soon dispelled, for I could see that the wind would carry the steamer past me, although, perhaps, at no great distance. Then my hopes sprang back to the boat hanging from her davits.

But before these hopes could take shape the woman and her glass died out of sight behind the rail of the steamer. In about a minute she reappeared, stood up erect, and applied a speaking-trumpet to her mouth. It was possible that a high, shrill voice might have been heard from one vessel to the other, but it was plain enough that this was a woman who took no useless chances. I, too, must be prepared to hail as well as to be hailed. Quickly I secured a speaking-trumpet from the captain's room, and stood up at my post.

Across the water came the monosyllable, "Ho!" and back I shouted, "Hallo!"

Then came these words, as clear and distinct as any I ever heard in my life: "Are you Mr. Rockwell?"

This question almost took away my senses. Was this reality? or had a spirit risen from this lonely ocean to summon me somewhere? Was this the way people died? Rockwell? Yes, my name was Rockwell. At least it had been. I was sure of nothing now.

Again came the voice across the sea. "Why don't you answer?" it said.

I raised my trumpet to my lips. At first I could make no sound, but, controlling my agitation a little, I shouted: "Yes!"

Instantly the woman disappeared, and for ten minutes I saw her no more. During that time I did nothing but stand and look at the steamer, which was moving more slowly than before, for the reason that the wind was dying away. She was now, however, nearly opposite me, and so near that if the wind should cease entirely, conversation might be held without the aid of trumpets. I earnestly hoped this might be the case, for I had now recovered the possession of my senses, and greatly desired to hear the natural voice of that young woman on the steamer.

As soon as she reappeared I made a trial of the power of my voice. Laying down the trumpet I shouted: "Who are you?"

Back came the answer, clear, high, and perfectly audible: "I am Mary Phillips."

Mary Phillips! it seemed to me that I remembered the name. I was certainly familiar with the erect attitude, and I fancied I recognized the features of the speaker. But this was all; I could not place her.

Before I could say anything she hailed again: "Don't you remember me?" she cried, "I lived in Forty-second Street."

The middle of a wild and desolate ocean and a voice from Forty-second Street! What manner of conjecture was this? I clasped my head in my hands and tried to think. Suddenly a memory came to me: a wild, surging, raging memory.

"With what person did you live in Forty-second Street?" I yelled across the water.

"Miss Bertha Nugent," she replied.

A fire seemed to blaze within me. Standing on tiptoe I fairly screamed: "Bertha Nugent! Where is she?"

The answer came back: "Here!" And when I heard it my legs gave way beneath me and I fell to the deck. I must have remained for some minutes half lying, half seated, on the deck. I was nearly stupefied by the statement I had heard.

I will now say a few words concerning Miss Bertha Nugent. She was a lady whom I had known well in New York, and who, for more than a year, I had loved well, although I never told her so. Whether or not she suspected my passion was a question about which I had never been able to satisfy myself. Sometimes I had one opinion; sometimes another. Before I had taken any steps to assure myself positively in regard to this point, Miss Nugent went abroad with a party of friends, and for eight months I had neither seen nor heard from her.

During that time I had not ceased to berate myself for my inexcusable procrastination. As she went away without knowing my feelings toward her, of course there could be no correspondence. Whatever she might have suspected, or whatever she might have expected, there was nothing between us.

But on my part my love for Bertha had grown day by day. Hating the city and even the country where I had seen her and loved her and where now she was not, I travelled here and there, and during the winter went to the West Indies. There I had remained until the weather had become too warm for a longer sojourn, and then I had taken passage in the *Thespia* for New York. I knew that Bertha would return to the city in the spring or summer, and I wished to be there

when she arrived. If, when I met her, I found her
free, there would be no more delay. My life thence-
forth would be black or white. And now here she
was near me in a half-wrecked steamer on the wide
Atlantic, with no companion, as I knew, but her maid,
Mary Phillips.

I now had a very distinct recollection of Mary
Phillips. In my visits to the Nugent household in
Forty-second Street I had frequently seen this young
woman. Two or three times when Miss Nugent had
not been at home, I had had slight interviews with
her. She always treated me with a certain cordiality,
and I had some reason to think that if Miss Nugent
really suspected my feelings, Mary Phillips had given
her some hints on the subject.

Mary Phillips was an exceedingly bright and quick
young woman, and I am quite sure that she could see
into the state of a man's feelings as well as any one.
Bertha had given me many instances of her maid's
facilities for adapting herself to circumstances, and I
was now thankful from the bottom of my heart that
Bertha had this woman with her.

I was recovering from the stupefaction into which
my sudden emotions had plunged me, when a hail
came across the water, first in Mary Phillips's natural
voice, and then through a speaking-trumpet. I stood
up and answered.

"I was wondering," cried Mary Phillips, "what
had become of you; I thought perhaps you had gone
down to breakfast." In answer I called to her to tell
me where Miss Nugent was, how she was, how she

came to be in this surprising situation, and how many people there were on board the steamer.

"Miss Nugent has not been at all well," answered Mary, "but she brightened up as soon as I told her you were here. She cannot come on deck very well, because the pitch of the ship makes the stairs so steep. But I am going to give her her breakfast now, and after she has eaten something she may be stronger, and I will try to get her on deck."

Brightened up when she knew I was near! That was glorious! That brightened up creation.

By this time I needed food also, but I did not remain below to eat it. I brought my breakfast on deck, keeping my eyes all the time fixed upon Bertha's steamer. The distance between us did not seem to have varied. How I longed for a little breeze that might bring us together! Bertha was on that vessel, trusting, perhaps, entirely to me: and what could I do if some breeze did not bring us together? I looked about for something on which I might float to her; but if I made a raft I was not sure that I could steer or propel it, and I might float away and become a third derelict. Once I thought of boldly springing into the water, and swimming to her; but the distance was considerable, my swimming powers were only moderate, and there might be sharks. The risk was too great. But surely we would come together. Even if no kind wind arose, there was that strange attraction which draws to each other the bubbles on a cup of tea. If bubbles, why not ships?

It was not long before nearly one-half of Mary

Phillips appeared above the rail. "Miss Nugent nas come on deck," she cried, "and she wants to see you. She can't stand up very long, because everything is so sliding."

Before my trembling lips could frame an answer, she had bobbed out of sight, and presently reappeared supporting another person, and that other person was Bertha Nugent.

I could discern her features perfectly. She was thinner and paler than when I had last seen her, but her beauty was all there. The same smile which I had seen so often was upon her face as she waved her handkerchief to me. I waved my hat in return, but I tried two or three times before I could speak loud enough for her to hear me. Then I threw into my words all the good cheer and hope that I could.

She did not attempt to answer, but smiled more brightly than before. Her expression seemed to indicate that, apart from the extraordinary pleasure of meeting a friend on this waste of waters, she was glad that I was that friend.

"She can't speak loud enough for you to hear her," called out Mary Phillips, "but she says that now you are here she thinks everything will be all right. She wants to know if you are alone on your ship, and if you can come to us."

I explained my situation, but said I did not doubt but the two ships would gradually drift together. "Is there no one to lower your boat?" I asked.

"No one but me," answered Mary, "and I don't believe I am up to that sort of thing. Miss Nugent

says _ must not touch it for fear I might fall over-
board."

"Do you mean to say," I cried, "that there is
nobody but you two on board that steamer ?"

"No other living soul!" said Mary, "and I'll tell
you how it all happened."

Then she told their story. The friends with whom
Miss Nugent had travelled had determined to go to
Egypt, but as she did not wish to accompany them,
she had remained in Spain and Algiers during the
early spring, and, eleven days before, she and Mary
Phillips had started from Marseilles for home in the
steamer *La Fidélité.* Five days ago, the steamer had
collided in the night with something, Mary did not
know what, and her front part was filled with water.
Everybody was sure that the vessel would soon sink,
and the captain, crew, and passengers — all French —
went away in boats.

"Is it possible " I yelled, "that they deserted you
two women ?"

Mary Phillips replied that this was not the case.
They had been implored to go in the boats, but the
night was dark, the sea was rough and pitchy, and
she was sure the boat would upset before they had
gone a hundred yards. Miss Nugent and she both
agreed that it was much safer to remain on a large
vessel like the *Fidélité,* even if she was half full of
water, than to go out on the dark and stormy water
in a miserable little shell of a boat. The captain got
down on his knees and implored them to go, but they
were resolute. He then declared that he would force

them into the craft, but Mary Phillips declared that if he tried that, she would shoot him; she had a pistol ready. Then, when they had all got in the boats but the captain, two of the men jumped on board again, threw their arms around him and carried him off, vowing that he should not lose his life on account of a pair of senseless Americans. A boat would be left, the men said, which they might use if they chose; but, of course, this was more a piece of sentiment than anything else.

"And now you see," cried Mary Phillips, "I was right, and they were wrong. This steamer has not sunk; and I have no manner of doubt that every soul who went away in those boats is now at the bottom of the sea."

This was indeed a wonderful story; and the fact that Bertha Nugent was on board a derelict vessel and should happen to fall in with me on board of another, was one of those events which corroborate the trite and hackneyed adage, that truth is stranger than fiction.

It was surprising how plainly I could hear Mary Phillips across the smooth, still water. The ships did not now seem to be moving at all; but soon they would be nearer, and then I could talk with Bertha. And soon after (it must be so) I would be with her.

I inquired if they had food and whatever else they needed; and Mary Phillips replied that, with the exception of the slanting position of the ship, they were very comfortable; that she did the cooking;

and that Miss Nugent said that they lived a great deal better than when the ship's cook cooked.

Mary also informed me that she had arranged a very nice couch for Miss Nugent on the afterdeck; that she was lying there now, and felt better; that she wanted to know which I thought the safer ship of the two; and that whenever a little wind arose, and the vessels were blown nearer each other, she wished to get up and talk to me herself.

I answered that I thought both the ships were safe enough, and should be delighted to talk with Miss Nugent, but in my heart I could not believe that a vessel with her bow as low as that of the *Fidélité* could be safe in bad weather, to say nothing of the possibility of, at any time, the water bursting into other compartments of the ship. The *Sparhawk* I believed to be in much better condition. Despite the fact that she was utterly helpless as far as sailing qualities were concerned, the greater part of her masts and rigging being in a wretched condition, and her rudder useless, she did not appear to be damaged. I had no reason to believe that she leaked, and she floated well, although, as I have said, she lay rather deep in the water.

If the thing were possible, I intended to get Bertha on board the *Sparhawk*, where there was hope that we could all remain safely until we were rescued. With this purpose in view, the moment Mary Phillips disappeared, I went below and prepared the captain's cabin for Bertha and her maid. I carried to the forward part of the vessel all the pipes, bottles, and glasses, and such other things as were not suitable for a lady's apartment, and thoroughly aired the cabin, making it as neat and comfortable as circumstances permitted. The very thought of offering hospitality to Bertha was a joy.

I proposed to myself several plans to be used in various contingencies. If the two vessels approached near enough, I would throw a line to *La Fidélité,* and Mary Phillips would make it fast, I knew. Then with a windlass I might draw the two vessels together. Then I would spring on board the steamer, and when I had transferred Bertha and Mary to the *Sparhawk,* would cut loose *La Fidélité* to drift where she pleased.

It was possible that I might convey from one vessel to the other some articles of luxury or necessity, but on this point I would not come to any definite conclusion. I would consult Mary Phillips on the subject.

Another plan was that if we did not approach very close, I would endeavor to throw a long, light line to the steamer, and Mary Phillips would attach it to the boat which hung from the davits. Into this she would put a pair of oars and lower it as well as she could; then I would haul it to the *Sparhawk,* row over to the steamer, and transfer Bertha and Mary to my vessel. It was possible that we should not have to be very near each other for me to carry out this plan. Had I been a seaman, I might have thought of some other plan better than these. But I was not a seaman.

I did not waste any time in the cabin, although I was very desirous to make it as pleasant as possible for the reception of Bertha, but when I returned to the deck I was astonished to find that the steamer was farther away than it had been when I went below. There was a slight breeze from the east, which had nearly turned the *Sparhawk* about with her bow to the wind, but was gently carrying *La Fidélité* before it.

I seized the speaking-trumpet, and with all my power, hailed the steamer; and in return there came to me a single sound, the sound of the vowel O. I could see two handkerchiefs fluttering upon the stern. In ten minutes these were scarcely discernible.

Half-crazed, I stood and gazed, and gazed, and gazed at the distant steamer. The wind died away, and I could perceive that she was not becoming more distant. Then I began to hope. Another wind might spring up which would bring her back.

And in an hour or two the other wind did spring up; I felt it in my face, and slowly the *Sparhawk* turned her bow toward it, and, enrapturing sight! the steamer, with my Bertha on board, began to move slowly back to me!

The wind which was now blowing came from the southwest, and *La Fidélité*, which before had lain to the southward of the *Sparhawk*, was passing to the north of my vessel. Nearer and nearer she came, and my whole soul was engaged in the hope that she might not pass too far north.

But I soon saw that unless the wind changed, the steamer would probably pass within hailing distance.

Soon I could see Mary Phillips on deck, speaking-trumpet in hand; and seizing my trumpet, I hailed

when as I thought we were near enough. I eagerly
inquired after Bertha, and the high voice of Mary
Phillips came across the water, telling me that Miss
Nugent was not feeling at all well. This uncertain
state of affairs was making her feel very nervous.
"Can she come on deck ? " I cried.  "Can she use a
speaking-trumpet ?  If I could talk to her, I might
encourage her."

"She needs it," answered Mary, "but she cannot
speak through the trumpet; she tried it, and it made
her head ache.  She is here on deck, and I am going
to help her stand up as soon as we get nearer.  Perhaps she may be able to speak to you."

The two vessels were now near enough for a high-
pitched conversation without the assistance of trumpets, and Mary Phillips assisted Bertha to the side
of the steamer, where I could distinctly see her.  I
shouted as hearty a greeting as ever was sent across
the water, bidding her to keep up a good heart, for
help of some kind must surely come to us.  She tried
to answer me, but her voice was not strong enough.
Then she shook her head, by which I understood that
she did not agree with me in my hopeful predictions.
I called back to her that in all this drifting about the
two vessels must certainly come together, and then,
with the assistance of the steamer's boat, we could
certainly devise some way of getting out of this an-
noying plight.  She smiled, apparently at the mildness
of this expression, and again shook her head.  She
now seemed tired, for her position by the rail was not
an easy one to maintain, and her maid assisted her to

her couch on the deck. Then stood up Mary Phillips, speaking loud and promptly : —

"She has a message for you," she said, "which she wanted to give to you herself, but she cannot do it. She thinks — but I tell her it is of no use thinking that way — that we are bound to be lost. You may be saved because your ship seems in a better condition than ours, and she does not believe that the two vessels will ever come together; so she wants me to tell you that if you get home and she never does, that she wishes her share in the Forty-second Street house to go to her married sister, and to be used for the education of the children. She doesn't want it divided up in the ordinary way, because each one will get so little, and it will do no good. Do you think that will be a good will?"

"Don't speak of wills!" I shouted; "there is no need of a will. She will get home in safety and attend to her own affairs."

"I think so, too," cried Mary Phillips; "but I had to tell you what she said. And now she wants to know if you have any message to send to your parents, for we might blow off somewhere and be picked up, while this might not happen to you. But I don't believe in that sort of thing any more than in the other."

I shouted back my disbelief in the necessity of any such messages, when Mary Phillips seized her trumpet and cried that she did not hear me.

Alas! the breeze was still blowing, and the steamer was moving away to the northeast. Through my

trumpet I repeated my words, and then Mary said
something which I could not hear. The wind was
against her. I shouted to her to speak louder, and
she must have screamed with all her force, but I
could only hear some words to the effect that we were
bound to come together again, and she waved her
handkerchief cheerily.

Then the steamer moved farther and farther away,
and speaking-trumpets were of no avail. I seized the
glass, and watched *La Fidélité* until she was nothing
but a black spot upon the sea.

The wind grew lighter, and finally died away, and
the black spot remained upon the horizon. I did not
take my eyes from it until night drew on and blotted
it out. I had not thought of advising Mary Phillips
to hang out a light, and she was probably not sufficiently accustomed to the ways of ships to think of
doing it herself, although there could be no doubt
that there were lanterns suitable for the purpose on
the steamer. Had there been a light upon that vessel,
I should have watched the glimmer all night. As it
was, I slept upon the deck, waking frequently to peer
out into the darkness, and to listen for a hail from a
speaking-trumpet.

In the morning there was a black spot upon the
horizon. I fancied that it was a little nearer than
when I last saw it; but in the course of the forenoon
it faded away altogether. Then despair seized upon
me, and I cared not whether I lived or died. I forgot
to eat, and threw myself upon the deck, where I remained for several hours, upbraiding myself for my

monstrous, unpardonable folly in neglecting the opportunities which were now lost.

Over and over again I told myself bitterly, that when I had been near enough to the vessel which bore Bertha Nugent to converse with Mary Phillips without the aid of a speaking-trumpet, I should have tried to reach that vessel, no matter what the danger or the difficulties. I should have launched a raft — I should have tried to swim — I should have done something.

And more than that, even had it been impossible for me to reach the steamer, I should have endeavored to reach Bertha's heart. I should have told her that I loved her. Whether she were lost or I were lost, or both of us, she should have known I loved her. She might not have been able to answer me, but she could have heard me. For that terrible mistake, that crime, there was no pardon. Now every chance was gone. What reason was there to suppose that these two derelicts ever again would drift together?

In the afternoon I rose languidly and looked about me. I saw something on the horizon, and seizing the glass, I knew it to be *La Fidélité*. I could recognize the slant of the hull, of the masts.

Now hope blazed up again. If she were nearer, she must come nearer still. I recovered my ordinary state of mind sufficiently to know that I was hungry, and that I must eat to be strong and ready for what might happen.

Upon one thing I was determined. If Bertha should ever again be brought near enough to hear me,

I would tell her that I loved her. The object of life, however much of it might be left me, should be to make Bertha know that I loved her. If I swam toward the vessel, or floated on a plank, I must get near enough to tell her that I loved her.

But there was no wind, and the apparent size of the steamer did not increase. This was a region or season of calms or fitful winds. During the rest of the day the distant vessel continued to be a black speck upon the smooth and gently rolling sea. Again I spent the night on deck, but I did not wake to listen or watch. I was worn out and slept heavily.

The day was bright when I was awakened by a chilly feeling: a strong breeze was blowing over me. I sprang to my feet. There was quite a heavy sea; the vessel was rolling and pitching beneath me, and not far away, not more than a mile, *La Fidélité* was coming straight toward me. Lightly laden, and with a great part of her hull high out of water, the high wind was driving her before it, while my vessel, her bow to the breeze, was moving at a much slower rate.

As I looked at the rapidly approaching steamer, it seemed as if she certainly must run into the *Sparhawk*. But for that I cared not. All that I now hoped for was that Bertha should come to me. Whether one vessel sank or the other, or whether both went down together, I should be with Bertha, I would live or die with her. Mary Phillips stood full in view on the stern of the oncoming steamer, a speaking-trumpet in her hand. I could now see that it was not probable that the two vessels would collide. The steamer would pass me, but probably very near. Before I could make up my mind what I should do in this momentous emergency, Mary Phillips hailed me.

"When we get near enough," she shouted, "throw me a rope. I'll tie it to the boat and cut it loose."

Wildly I looked about me for a line which I might throw. Cordage there was in abundance, but it was broken or fastened to something, or too heavy to handle. I remembered, however, seeing a coil of small rope below, and hastening down, I brought it on deck, took the coil in my right hand, and stood ready to hurl it when the proper moment should come.

That moment came quickly. The steamer was not a hundred feet from me when I reached the deck. It passed me on the port side.

"Be ready!" cried Mary Phillips, the instant she saw me. It was not now necessary to use a trumpet.

"Throw as soon as I get opposite to you!" she cried.

"Is Bertha well?" I shouted.

"Yes!" said Mary Phillips; "but what you've got to do is to throw that rope. Give it a good heave. Throw now!"

The two vessels were not fifty feet apart. With all my strength I hurled the coil of rope. The steamer's stern was above me, and I aimed high. The flying coil went over the deck of *La Fidélité*, but in my excitement I forgot to grasp tightly the other end of it, and the whole rope flew from me and disappeared beyond the steamer. Stupefied by this deplorable

accident, I staggered backward and a heave of the
vessel threw me against the rail. Recovering myself,
I glared about for another rope, but of course there
was none.

Then came a shout from Mary Phillips. But she
had already passed me, and as I was to the windward
of her I did not catch her words. As I remembered
her appearance, she seemed to be tearing her hair.
In a flash I thought of my resolution. Rushing to
the rail, I put the trumpet to my mouth. The wind
would carry my words to her if it would not bring
hers to me.

"Tell Bertha to come on deck!" I shouted. Mary
Phillips looked at me, but did not move. I wished
her to rush below and bring up Bertha. Not an instant was to be lost. But she did not move.

"Tell her I love her!" I yelled through the trumpet. "Tell her that I love her now and shall love her
forever. Tell her I love her, no matter what happens.
Tell her I love her, I love her, I love her!" And
this I continued to scream until it was plain I was no
longer heard. Then I threw down my useless trumpet
and seized the glass. Madly I scanned the steamer.
No sign of Bertha was to be seen. Mary Phillips was
there, and now she waved her handkerchief. At all
events she forgave me. At such a terrible moment
what could one do but forgive?

I watched, and watched, and watched, but no figure
but that of Mary Phillips appeared upon the steamer,
and at last I could not even distinguish that. Now I
became filled with desperate fury. I determined to

sail after Bertha and overtake her. A great sail was flapping from one of my masts, and I would put my ship about, and the strong wind should carry me to Bertha.

I knew nothing of sailing, but even if I had known, all my efforts would have been useless. I rushed to the wheel and tried to move it, pulling it this way and that, but the rudder was broken or jammed, — I know not what had happened to it. I seized the ropes attached to the boom of the sail, I pulled, I jerked, I hauled; I did not know what I was doing. I did nothing. At last, in utter despair and exhaustion, I fell to the deck.

But before the wind had almost died away, and in the afternoon the sea was perfectly calm, and when the sun set I could plainly see the steamer on the far-off edge of the glistening water. During the whole of the next day I saw her. She neither disappeared nor came nearer. Sometimes I was in the depths of despair; sometimes I began to hope a little; but I had one great solace in the midst of my misery — Bertha knew that I loved her. I was positively sure that my words had been heard.

It was a strange manner in which I had told my love. I had roared my burning words of passion through a speaking-trumpet, and I had told them not to Bertha herself, but to Mary Phillips. But the manner was of no importance. Bertha now knew that I loved her. That was everything to me.

As long as light remained I watched *La Fidélité* through the glass, but I could see nothing but a black

form with a slanting upper line. She was becalmed
as I was. Why could she not have been becalmed
near me? I dared not let my mind rest upon the
opportunities I had lost when she had been becalmed
near me. During the night the wind must have risen
again, for the *Sparhawk* rolled and dipped a good
deal, troubling my troubled slumbers. Very early in
the morning I was awakened by what sounded like a
distant scream. I did not know whether it was a
dream or not; but I hurried on deck. The sun had
not risen, but as I looked about I saw something
which took away my breath; which made me wonder
if I were awake, or dreaming, or mad.

It was Bertha's steamer within hailing distance!

Above the rail I saw the head and body of Mary
Phillips, who was screaming through the trumpet. I
stood and gazed in petrified amazement.

I could not hear what Mary Phillips said. Perhaps
my senses were benumbed. Perhaps the wind was
carrying away her words. That it was blowing from
me toward her soon became too evident. The steamer
was receding from the *Sparhawk*. The instant I
became aware of this my powers of perception and
reasoning returned to me with a burning flash.

Bertha was going away from me — she was almost
gone.

Snatching my trumpet, I leaned over the rail and
shouted with all my might: "Did you hear me say I
loved her? Did you tell her?"

Mary Phillips had put down her trumpet, but now
she raised it again to her mouth, and I could see that

she was going to make a great effort. The distance between us had increased considerably since I came on deck, and she had to speak against the wind.

With all the concentrated intensity which high-strung nerves could give to a man who is trying to hear the one thing to him worth hearing in the world, I listened. Had a wild beast fixed his claws and teeth into me at the moment I would not have withdrawn my attention.

I heard the voice of Mary Phillips, faint, far away. I heard the words, "Yes, but —" and the rest was lost. She must have known from my aspect that her message did not reach me, for she tried again and again to make herself heard.

The wind continued to blow, and the steamer continued to float and float and float away. A wind had come up in the night. It had blown Bertha near me; perhaps it had blown her very near me. She had not known it, and I had not known it. Mary Phillips had not known it until it was too late, and now that wind had blown her past me and was blowing her away. For a time there was a flutter of a handkerchief, but only one handkerchief, and then *La Fidélité*, with Bertha on board, was blown away until she disappeared, and I never saw her again.

All night I sat upon the deck of the *Sparhawk*, thinking, wondering, and conjecturing. I was in a strange state of mind. I did not wonder or conjecture whether Bertha's vessel would come back to me again; I did not think of what I should do if it did come back. I did not think of what I should do if it never came back. All night I thought, wondered, and conjectured what Mary Phillips had meant by the word "but."

It was plain to me what "yes" had meant. My message had been heard, and I knew Mary Phillips well enough to feel positively sure that having received such a message under such circumstances she had given it to Bertha. Therefore I had positive proof that Bertha knew that I loved her. But what did the "but" mean?

It seemed to me that there were a thousand things that this word might mean. It might mean that she was already engaged to be married. It might mean that she had vowed never to marry. It might mean that she disapproved of such words at such a time. I cannot repeat the tenth of the meanings which I thought I might attach to this word. But the worst thing that it could purport, the most terrible signification of all, recurred to me over and over again. It might mean that Bertha could not return my affection. She knew that I loved her, but she could not love me.

In the morning I ate something and then lay down upon the deck to sleep. It was well that I should do this, I thought, because if Bertha came near me again in the daytime Mary Phillips would hail me if I were not awake. All night long I would watch, and, as there was a moon, I would see Bertha's vessel if it came again.

I did watch all that afternoon and all that night, and during my watching I never ceased to wonder and conjecture what Mary Phillips meant by that word "but."

About the middle of the next day I saw in the distance something upon the water. I first thought it a bit of spray, for it was white, but as there were now no waves there could be no spray. With the glass I could only see that it was something white shining in the sun. It might be the glistening body of a dead fish. After a time it became plainer to me. It was such a little object that the faint breezes which occasionally arose had more influence upon the *Sparhawk* than upon it, and so I gradually approached it.

In about an hour I made out that it was something round, with something white raised above it, and then I discovered that it was a life-preserver, which supported a little stick, to which a white flag, probably a handkerchief, was attached. Then I saw that on the life-preserver lay a little yellow mass.

Now I knew what it was that I saw. It was a message from Bertha. Mary Phillips had devised the means of sending it. Bertha had sent it.

The life-preserver was a circular one, filled with air. In the centre of this, Mary, by means of many strings, had probably secured a stick in an upright position; she had then fastened a handkerchief to the top of the stick. Bertha had written a message and Mary had wrapped it in a piece of oiled silk and fastened it to the life-preserver. She had then lowered this contrivance to the surface of the water, hoping that it would float to me or I would float to it.

I was floating to it. It contained the solution of all my doubts, the answer to all my conjectures. It was Bertha's reply to my declaration of love, and I

was drifting slowly but surely toward it. Soon I
would know.

But after a time the course of the *Sparhawk* or the
course of the message changed. I drifted to the
north. Little by little my course deviated from the
line on which I might have met the message. At last
I saw that I should never meet it. When I became
convinced of this, my first impulse was to spring over-
board and swim for it. But I restrained this impulse,
as I had restrained others like it. If Bertha came
back, I must be ready to meet her. I must run no
risks, for her sake and my sake. She must find me
on the *Sparhawk* if she should come back. She had
left me and she had come back; she might come back
again. Even to get her message I must not run the
risk of missing her. And so with yearning heart and
perhaps tearful eyes I watched the little craft disappear and become another derelict.

I do not know how many days and nights I watched
and waited for Bertha's ship and wondered and conjectured what Mary Phillips meant by "but." I was
awake so much and ate so little and thought so hard
that I lost strength, both of mind and body. All
I asked of my body was to look out for Bertha's
steamer, and all that I asked of my mind was to re-
solve the meaning of the last words I had heard from
that vessel.

One day, I do not know whether it was in the morning or afternoon, I raised my head, and on the horizon
I saw a steamer. Quick as a flash my glass was
brought to bear upon it. In the next minute my arms

dropped, the telescope fell into my lap, my head dropped. It was not Bertha's steamer; it was an ordinary steamer with its deck parallel with the water and a long line of smoke coming out of its funnel. The shock of the disappointment was very great.

When I looked up again I could see that the steamer was headed directly toward me, and was approaching with considerable rapidity. But this fact affected me little. It would not bring me Bertha. It would not bring me any message from her. It was an ordinary vessel of traffic. I took no great interest in it, one way or the other.

Before long it was so near that I could see people on board. I arose and looked over the rail. Then some one on the steamer fired a gun or a pistol. As this seemed to be a signal, I waved my hat. Then the steamer began to move more slowly, and soon lay to and lowered a boat.

In ten minutes three men stood on the deck of the *Sparhawk.* Some one had hailed me in English to lower something. I had lowered nothing; but here they were on deck. They asked me a lot of questions, but I answered none of them.

"Is your captain with you?" I said. They answered that he was not, that he was on the steamer. "Then take me to him," said I.

"Of course we will," said their leader, with a smile. And they took me.

I was received on the steamer with much cordiality and much questioning, but to none of it did I pay any attention. I addressed the captain.

"Sir," said I, "I will be obliged to you if you will immediately cruise to the southwest and pick up for me a life-preserver with a little white flag attached to it. It also carries a message for me, wrapped up in a piece of oiled silk. It is very important that I should obtain that message without delay."

The captain laughed. "Why, man!" said he, "what are you thinking of? Do you suppose that I can go out of my course to cruise after a life-preserver?"

I looked at him with scorn. "Unmanly fiend!" said I.

Another officer now approached, whom I afterward knew to be the ship's doctor.

"Come, come now," he said, "don't let us have any hard words. The captain is only joking. Of course he will steam after your life-preserver, and no doubt will come up with it very soon. In the meantime you must come below and have something to eat and drink and rest yourself."

Satisfied with this assurance, I went below, was given food and medicine, and was put into a berth, where I remained for four days in a half-insensible condition, knowing nothing — caring for nothing.

When I came on deck again I was very weak, but I had regained my senses, and the captain and I talked rationally together. I told him how I had come on board the *Sparhawk*, and how I had fallen in with the *La Fidélité*, half wrecked, having on board only a dear friend of mine. In answer to his questions I described the details of the communications between the two

vessels, and could not avoid mentioning the wild hopes
and heart-breaking disappointments of that terrible
time. And, somewhat to my languid surprise, the
captain asked no questions regarding these subjects.
I finished by thanking him for having taken me from
the wreck, but added that I felt like a false-hearted
coward for having deserted upon the sea the woman I
loved, who now would never know my fate nor I hers.

"Don't be too sure of that," said the captain, "for
you are about to hear from her now."

I gazed at him in blank amazement. "Yes," said
the captain, "I have seen her, and she has sent me to
you. But I see you are all knocked into a heap, and
I will make the story as short as I can. This vessel
of mine is bound from Liverpool to La Guayra, and
on the way down we called at Lisbon. On the morning of the day I was to sail from there, there came into
port the *Glanford*, a big English merchantman, from
Buenos Ayres to London. I knew her skipper, Captain Guy Chesters, as handsome a young English sailor
as ever stood upon a deck.

"In less than an hour from the time we dropped
anchor, Captain Guy was on my vessel. He was on
the lookout, he said, for some craft bound for South
America or the West Indies, and was delighted to
find me there. Then he told me that, ten days before,
he had taken two ladies from a half-wrecked French
steamer, and that they had prayed and besought him
to cruise about and look for the *Sparhawk*, a helpless
ship, with a friend of theirs alone on board.

"'You know,' said Captain Guy to me, 'I couldn't

do that, for I'd lost time enough already, and the wind was very light and variable; so all I could do was to vow to the ladies that when we got to Lisbon we'd be bound to find a steamer going south, and that she could easily keep a lookout for the *Sparhawk,* and take off the friend.' 'That was a pretty big contract you marked out for the steamer going south,' I said, 'and as for the *Sparhawk,* she's an old derelict, and I sighted her on my voyage north, and sent in a report of her position, and there couldn't have been anybody on board of her then.' 'Can't say,' said Captain Guy; 'from what I can make out, this fellow must have boarded her a good while after she was abandoned, and seems to have been lying low after that.' Was that so, sir? Did you lie low?"

I made no answer. My whole soul was engaged in the comprehension of the fact that Bertha had sent for me. "Go on!" I cried.

"All right," said he. "I ought not to keep you waiting. I promised Captain Guy I would keep a lookout for the *Sparhawk,* and take you off if you were on board. I promised the quicker, because my conscience was growling at me for having, perhaps, passed a fellow-being on an abandoned vessel. But I had heard of the *Sparhawk* before. I had sighted her, and so didn't keep a very sharp lookout for living beings aboard. Then Captain Guy took me on board his ship to see the two ladies, for they wanted to give me instructions themselves. And I tell you what, sir, you don't often see two prettier women on board ship, nor anywhere else, for that matter. Captain

Guy told me that before I saw them. He was in great spirits about his luck. He is the luckiest fellow in the merchant service. Now, if I had picked up two people that way, it would have been two old men. But he gets a couple of lovely ladies; that's the way the world goes. The ladies made me pretty nigh swear that I'd never set foot on shore till I found you. I would have been glad enough to stay there all day and make promises to those women; but my time was short, and I had to leave them to Captain Guy. So I did keep a lookout for the *Sparhawk,* and heard of her from two vessels coming north, and finally fell in with you. And a regular lunatic you were when I took you on board; but that's not to be wondered at; and you seem to be all right now."

"Did you not bring me any message from them?" I asked.

"Oh, yes; lots," said the captain. "Let me see if I can remember some of them." And then he knit his brows and tapped his head, and repeated some very commonplace expressions of encouragement and sympathy.

The effect of these upon me was very different from what the captain had expected. I had hoped for a note, a line — anything direct from Bertha. If she had written something which would explain the meaning of those last words from Mary Phillips, whether that explanation were favorable or otherwise, I would have been better satisfied; but now my terrible suspense must continue.

"Well," said the captain, "you don't seem cheered

up much by word from your friends. I was too busy looking at them to rightly catch everything they said, but I know they told me they were going to London in the *Glanford.* This I remembered, because it struck me what a jolly piece of good luck it all was for Captain Guy."

"And for what port are you bound?" I asked. "La Guayra," he said. "It isn't a very good time of the year to be there; but I don't doubt that you can find some vessel or other there that will take you north, so you're all right."

I was not all right. Bertha was saved. I was saved; but I had received no message. I knew nothing; and I was going away from her.

Two or three days after this, the captain came to me and said: "Look here, young man; you seem to be in the worst kind of doleful dumps. People who have been picked up in the middle of the ocean don't generally look like that. I wonder if you're not a little love-sick on account of a young woman on the *Glanford.*"

I made no answer; I would not rebuke him, for he had saved my life; but this was a subject which I did not wish to discuss with a sea-captain.

"If that's really what's the matter with you," said he, "I can give you a piece of advice which will do you good if you take it. I think you told me that you are not engaged to this lady," (I nodded) "and that you never proposed to her except through a speaking-trumpet." I allowed silence to make assent. "Well, now, my advice is to give her up, to drop all thoughts

of her, and to make up your mind to tackle onto some
other girl when you find one that is good enough.
You haven't the least chance in the world with this
one. Captain Guy is mad in love with her. He told
me so himself, and when he's out and out in love with
a girl he's bound to get her. When I was with him
he might have been married once a month if he'd
chosen to; but he didn't choose. Now he does choose,
and I can tell you that he's not going to make love
through a speaking-trumpet. He'll go straight at it,
and he'll win, too. There's every reason why he
should win. In the first place, he's one of the hand-
somest fellows, and I don't doubt one of the best love-
makers that you would be likely to meet on land or
sea. And then again, she has every reason to be grateful to him and to look on him as a hero."

I listened without a word. The captain's reasoning
seemed to me very fallacious.

"You don't know it," said he, "but Captain Guy
did a good deal more than pick up those two women
from an abandoned vessel. You see he was making
his way north with a pretty fair wind from the southwest, the first they'd had for several days, and when
his lookout sighted *La Fidélité* nobody on board
thought for a minute that he would try to beat up
to her, for she lay a long way to the west of his
course, though pretty well in sight.

"But Captain Guy has sharp eyes and a good glass,
and he vowed that he could see something on the
wreck that looked like a handkerchief waved by a
woman. He told me this himself as we were walking

from my ship to his.  Everybody laughed at him and
wanted to know if women waved handkerchiefs different from other people.

"They said that any bit of canvas might wave like
that, and that it was plain enough that the vessel was
abandoned.  If it was not, it could be, for there was a
boat still hanging to one of its davits.  Captain Guy
paid no attention to this, but spied a little longer;
then he vowed that he was going to make for that
vessel.  There was one of the owners on board, and
he up and forbid Captain Guy to do it.  He told him
that they had been delayed enough on the voyage by
light winds, and now that they would be over-due at
their port a good many days before they got there.
Every day lost, he said, was money lost to the owners.
He had never heard of any skipper undertaking a
piece of tomfoolery like this.  It would take all day
to beat up to that wreck, and when they reached it
they would find an old derelict, which was no more
than they could see now.  And as for there being a
woman on board, that was all stuff.  The skipper had
woman on the brain.

"To this Captain Guy answered that he didn't own
the ship, but he commanded her, and as long as he
commanded this vessel or any other, he was not going
to pass a wreck when there were good reasons to
believe that there was a human being on board of
it, and in spite of what anybody said, his eyes told
him that there was reason to believe that there was
somebody waving on that wreck.  So he ordered the
ship put about, paying no attention to the cursing and

swearing of the owner, and beat against a wind that was getting lighter and lighter for over four hours until he reached the French steamer and took off the two ladies.

"There was nobody on board the *Glanford* that thinks that Captain Guy will ever sail that ship again. And in fact he don't think so himself. But said he to me: "If I can marry that girl, the ship can go. If I can't get another ship, I can sail under a skipper. But there's no other girl in the world like this one.""

"And so you see, sir," he continued, "there isn't the least chance in the world for you. Captain Guy's got her on board his ship; he's with her by sunlight and starlight. He's lost his ship for her and he wants to marry her. And on the other hand, it'll be weeks and weeks and perhaps months before you can see her, or write to her either, as like as not, and long before that Captain Guy will have his affair settled, and there isn't any reason in my mind to doubt which way it will settle. And so you just take my advice, sir, and stop drawing that long face. There are plenty of good girls in the world; no reason why you shouldn't get one; but if you are moping for the one that Captain Guy's got his heart set on, I'm afraid you'll end by being as much out of your head as you were when I found you."

To all this I made no answer, but walked gloomily toward the stern and looked down into the foaming wake. I think I heard the captain tell one of the men to keep an eye on me.

When we reached La Guayra — and the voyage seemed to me a never-ending one — I immediately set about finding a vessel bound for England. My captain advised me to go up on the mountains and wait until a steamer should sail for New York, which event might be expected in two or three weeks. America would be much better for me, he thought, than would England. But I paid no attention to him, and as there was nothing in port that would sail for England, I took passage in a Spanish steamer bound for Barcelona. Arriving there, after a passage long enough to give me plenty of time for the consideration of the last two words I heard from Mary Phillips, and of the value of the communications I had received regarding Captain Guy Chesters, I immediately started by rail for London. On this journey I found that what I had heard concerning the rescue of my Bertha had had a greater effect upon me than I had supposed. Trains could not go fast enough for me. I was as restless as a maniac; I may have looked like one.

Over and over I tried to quiet myself by comforting reflections, saying to myself, for instance, that if the message which Bertha had sent floating on the sea to me had not been a good one, she would not have sent it. Feel as she might, she could not have been so hard-hearted as to crush the hopes of a man who, like herself, might soon lie in a watery grave. But then, there was that terrible word "but." Looked at in certain lights, what could be more crushing or heart-breaking than that?

And then again, Mary Phillips may not have understood what I said to her through the speaking-trumpet. A grim humor of despair suggested that at that distance, and in that blustering wind, the faithful maid-servant might have thought that instead of shouting that I loved my Bertha, I was asking her if they had plenty of salt pork and hardtack. It was indeed a time of terrible suspense.

I did not know Bertha's address in England. I knew that she had friends in London and others in the country; but I was sure that I would find her if she were on the island. I arrived in London very early in the morning, too early to expect to find open any of the banking-houses or other places where Americans would be likely to register. Unable to remain inactive, I took a cab and drove to the London docks.

I went to inquire the whereabouts of Captain Guy Chesters.

This plan of action was almost repulsive to me, but I felt that it offered an opportunity which I should not neglect. I would certainly learn about Bertha if I saw him, and whether it would be anything good or anything bad I ought to know it.

In making my inquiries the cabman was of much assistance to me. And after having been referred from one person to another, I at last found a man, first mate of a vessel in the docks, who knew Captain Chesters, and could tell me all about him.

"Yes, sir," said he, "I can tell you where to find Captain Chesters. He's on shore, for he doesn't command the *Glanford* now, and as far as I know he hasn't signed articles yet either as skipper or mate in any other craft. The fact is, he's engaged in business, which I suppose he thinks better than sailing the sea. He was married about a month ago. It's only two or three days since he's got back from a little land trip they took on the Continent. I saw him yesterday; he's the happiest man alive. But it's as like as not that he's ready for business now that he's got through with his honeymoon, and if it's a skipper you're looking for you can't find a better man than Captain Guy, not about these docks."

I stood and looked at the man without seeing him, and then in a hollow voice asked: "Where does he live?"

"A hundred and nine Lisbury Street, Calistoy Road, East. Now that I've told you, I wish I hadn't. You look as though you were going to measure him for a coffin."

"Thank you," said I, and walked away.

I told the cabman to drive me to the address I had received, and in due time we arrived in front of a very good-looking house, in a quiet and respectable street.

I was in a peculiar state of mind. I had half expected the terrible shock, and I had received it. But I had not been stunned; I had been roused to an unusual condition of mental activity. My senses were sharpened by the torment of my soul, and I observed everything, — the quarter of the city, the street, the house.

The woman who opened the door started a little

when she saw me. I asked for Mrs. Captain Chesters, and walked in without waiting to be told whether the lady was in or not. The woman showed me into a little parlor, and left me. Her manner plainly indicated that she suspected something was the matter with me.

In a very short time a tall, well-made man, with curly brown hair, a handsome, sun-browned face, and that fine presence which command at sea frequently gives, entered the room.

"I understand, sir," said he, "that you asked for my wife, but I thought it better to come to you myself. What is your business with her, sir, and what is your name?"

"My name is Charles Rockwell," I said, "and my business is to see her. If she has already forgotten my name, you can tell her that I kept company with her for a while on the Atlantic Ocean, when she was in one wreck and I was in another."

"Good heavens!" cried the young sailor; "do you mean to say that you are the man who was on the derelict *Sparhawk?* And were you picked up by Captain Stearns, whom I sent after you? I supposed he would have written to me about you."

"I came faster than a letter would come," I answered. "Can I see her?"

"Of course you can!" cried Captain Guy. "I never knew a man so talked about as you have been since I fell in with the wreck of that French steamer! By George! sir, there was a time when I was dead jealous of you. But I'm married tight and fast now, and that sort of thing is done with. Of course you shall see her."

He left the room, and presently I heard the sound of running footsteps. The door was opened, and Mary Phillips entered, closely followed by the captain. I started back; I shouted as if I had a speaking-trumpet to my mouth : —

"What!" I cried; "is this your wife ? "

"Yes," said Captain Guy, stepping forward, "of course she is. Why not ? "

I made no answer, but, with open arms I rushed upon Mary Phillips and folded her in a wild embrace. I heard a burst of nautical oaths, and probably would have been felled by a nautical fist, had not Mary screamed to her husband : —

"Stop, Guy !" she cried; "I understand him. It's all right. He's so glad to see me."

I released her from my embrace, and, staggering back, sank upon a chair.

"Go get him a glass of sherry, Guy," she said, and wheeling up a great easy-chair, she told me to sit in it, for I looked dreadfully tired. I took the chair, and when the wine was brought I drank it.

"Where is Miss Nugent ? " I asked.

"Miss Nugent is all right," said Mary Phillips, "but I'm not going to tell you a word about her or anything else until you've had some breakfast. I know you have not tasted food this day."

I admitted that I had not. I would eat, I would do anything, so that afterward she would tell me about Bertha.

When I had a cup of coffee and some toast which Mary brought to me upon a tray, I arose from my chair.

"Now tell me quickly," I said, "where is Bertha?"

"Not a bit of it," said Mary Phillips — I call her so, for I shall never know her by any other name.

"Sit down again, Mr. Rockwell, and eat these two eggs. When you have done that I will talk to you about her. You needn't be in a hurry to go to see her, because in the house where she is the people are not up yet."

"Might as well sit down and eat," said the captain, laughing. "When you're under command of this skipper you will find that her orders are orders, and the quicker you step up and obey them, the better. So I would advise you to eat your eggs."

I began to do so, and Captain Guy laughed a mighty laugh. "She's a little thing," he said, "but she does know how to make men stand about. I didn't believe there was a person in this world who could have kept my hands off you when I saw you hugging my wife. But she did it, and I tell you, sir, I was never worse cut up in my whole life than I was when I saw you do that."

"Sir," said I, looking at him steadfastly, "if I have caused you any pain, any misery, any torment of the soul, any anguish of heart, any agony of jealousy, or mental torture of any kind, I am heartily glad of it, for all of these things you have brought on me."

"Good!" cried Mary Phillips; "you must be feeling better, sir, and when you have entirely finished breakfast we will go on and talk."

In a few moments I pushed away the tray, and Mary, looking at it, declared herself satisfied, and placed it on a side table.

"So you really supposed, sir," she said, sitting near me, "that Captain Chesters married Miss Nugent?"

"I certainly did," I answered.

"No doubt, thinking," said Mary, with a smile, "that no man in his senses would marry anybody else when Miss Nugent was about, which was a very proper opinion, of course, considering your state of mind."

"And let me say, sir," said Captain Guy, "if I had married Miss Nugent, more people than you would have been dissatisfied. I would have been one of them, and I am sure Miss Nugent would have been another."

"Count me as one of that party," said Mary Phillips. "And now, Mr. Rockwell, you shall not be kept waiting a moment longer."

"Of course she is safe and well," I said, "or you you would not be here, and before you say anything more about her, please tell me what you meant by that terrible word 'but.'"

"But?" repeated Mary Phillips, with a puzzled expression. And Captain Guy echoed, "But? What but?"

"It was the last word I heard from you," said I; "you shouted it to me when your vessel was going away for the last time. It has caused me a world of misery. It may have been followed by other words, but I did not catch them. I asked you if you had told her that I loved her, and you answered, 'Yes, but —'"

Captain Guy slapped his leg, "By George!" he said; "that was enough to put a man on the rack. Mary, you should have told him more than that."

Mary Phillips wrinkled her forehead and gazed steadfastly into her lap. Suddenly she looked up.

"I remember it," she said; "I remember exactly what I answered or tried to answer. I said, 'Yes, but she knew it before.'"

I sprang to my feet. "What do you mean?" I cried.

"Of course she knew it," she cried: "we must both have been very stupid if we hadn't known that. We knew it before we left New York; and, for my part, I wondered why you didn't tell her. But as you never mentioned it, of course it wasn't for us to bring up the subject."

"Bertha knew I loved her?" I ejaculated. "And what — and how — what did she say of it? What did she think of it?"

"Well," said Mary Phillips, laughing, "I could never see that she doubted it; I could never see that she objected to it. In fact, from what she said, and, being just us two, of course she had to say a good many things to me, I think she was very glad to find out that you knew it as well as we did."

"Mary Phillips!" I cried; "where is she? Tell me this moment!"

"Look here," said Captain Guy, "you're leaving me out of this business altogether. This is Mrs. Mary Chesters."

"Mr. Rockwell will be all right when he gets over this flurry," said Mary to her husband.

I acknowledged the correction with a nod, for I had no time then for words on the subject.

"Don't get yourself flustered, sir," said Mary. "You can't go to her yet; it's too early. You must give the family time to come down and have breakfast. I am not going to be party to a scene before breakfast nor in the middle of a meal. I know the ways and manners of that house, and I'll send you at exactly the right time."

I sat down. "Mary — Mrs. —"

"Don't bother about names just now," she interrupted; "I know who you're speaking to."

"Do you believe," I continued, looking steadfastly at her, "that Bertha Nugent loves me?"

"I don't know," she said, "that it's exactly my business to give this information, but under the circumstances I take it on myself to say that she most certainly does. And I tell you, and you may tell her if you like, that I would not have said this to you if I hadn't believed this thing ought to be clinched the minute there was a chance to do it. It's been hanging off and on long enough. Love you? Why, bless my soul, sir, she's been thinking of nothing else for the past two or three days but the coming of the postman, expecting a letter from you, not considering that you didn't know where to address her, or that it was rather scant time for a letter to come from La Guayra, where Captain Stearns would take you if he succeeded in picking you up."

"The whole affair had a scanty air about it," said Captain Guy. "At least, that's the way I look at it."

"You've never said anything like that before," said Mary, rather sharply.

"Of course not," replied the captain. "I wanted to keep you as merry and cheerful as I could. And besides, I didn't say I had thought there was no chance of Mr. Rockwell's turning up. I only said I considered it a little scantish."

"Love you?" continued Mary Phillips; "I should say so. I should have brought her on deck to wave her handkerchief to you and kiss her hand — perhaps, when you blew the state of your feelings through a trumpet; but she wasn't strong enough. She was a pretty weak woman in body and mind about that time. But from the moment I told her, and she knew that you not only loved her, but were willing to say so, she began to mend. And how she did talk about you, and how she did long that the two ships might come together again! She kept asking me what I thought about the condition of your vessel and whether it would be like to sink if a storm came on. I could not help thinking that, as far as I knew anything about ships, you'd be likely to float for weeks after we'd gone down, but I didn't say that to her. And then she began to wonder if you had understood that she had received your message and was glad to get it. And I told her over and over and over again that you must have heard me, for I screamed my very loudest. I am very glad that I didn't know that you only caught those two words."

"Dear girl!" I ejaculated. "And did she send me a message on a life-preserver?"

"You mean to say that you got it?" cried Mary Phillips.

"No," said I; "it floated away from me. What was it?"

"I got up that little scheme," said Mary Phillips, "to quiet her. I told her that a letter might be floated to you that way, and that, anyway, it would do no harm to try. I don't know what she wrote, but she must have said a good deal, for she took a long time about it. I wrapped it up perfectly water-tight. She made the flag herself out of one of her own handkerchiefs with her initial in the corner. She said she thought you would like that."

"Oh, that it had come to me!" I cried.

"I wish from the bottom of my soul that it had," said Mary, compassionately. "It would have done you a lot of good on that lonely ship."

"Instead of which," observed Captain Guy, "some shark probably swallowed it, and little good it did him."

"It put a lot of affection and consideration into him," said Mary, a little brusquely, "and there are other creatures connected with the sea who wouldn't be hurt by that sort of thing."

"There's a shot into me!" cried the captain. "Don't do it again. I cry quarter!"

"I must go," I said, rising; "I can wait no longer."

"Well," said Mary, "you may not be much too soon, if you go slowly."

"But before I go," I said, "tell me this: Why did she not send me some word from Lisbon? Why did she not give Captain Stearns a line on a piece of paper or some message?"

"A line! a message!" exclaimed Mary. "She sent you a note; she sent you a dozen messages by Captain Stearns."

"And I'll wager a month's pay," said Captain Guy, "that he never delivered one of them."

"He gave me no note," I cried.

"It's in the pocket of his pea-jacket now," said Captain Chesters.

"He did deliver some messages," I said, "after I questioned him; but they were such as these: Keep up a good heart; everything's bound to be right in the end; the last to get back gets the heartiest welcome. Now, anybody could have sent such words as those."

"Upon my word," cried Mary Phillips, "those were the messages I sent. I remember particularly the one about the last one back and the heartiest welcome."

"Confound that Stearns!" cried Captain Guy; "what did he mean by giving all his attention to you, and none to the lady that he was sent for to see?"

"Good bye, Mrs. Chesters," I said, taking her by the hand. "I can never thank you enough for what you have done for her and for me. But how you could leave her I really do not understand."

"Well," said Mary, coloring a little, "I can scarcely understand it myself; but that man would have it so, and he's terribly obstinate. But I don't feel that I've left her. She's in the best of hands, and I see her nearly every day. Here's her address, and when you meet her, Mr. Rockwell, you'll find that in every way I've told you truly."

I took a hearty leave of Captain Guy, shook Mary by the hand once more, rushed down stairs, roused the sleeping cabby, and glancing at the card, ordered him to gallop to 9 Ravisdock Terrace, Parmley Square.

I do not know how I got into the house, what I said nor what I asked, nor whether the family had had their breakfast or not; but the moment my eyes fell upon my beloved Bertha I knew that in everything Mary Phillips had told me truly. She came into the room with beaming eyes and both hands extended. With outstretched arms I rushed to meet her, and folded her to my breast. This time there was no one to object. For some moments we were speechless with joyful emotion, but there was no need of our saying anything, no need of statements nor explanations. Mary Phillips had attended to all that.

When we had cooled down to the point of speech, I was surprised to find that I had been expected, that Bertha knew I was coming. When Mary Phillips had left me that morning to prepare my breakfast, she had sent a message to Bertha, and then she had detained me until she thought it had been received and Bertha was prepared to meet me.

"I did not want any slips or misses," she said, when she explained the matter to me afterward. "I don't want to say anything about your personal appearance, Mr. Rockwell, but there are plenty of servants in

London who, if they hadn't had their orders, would shut the door in the face of a much less wild-eyed person than you were, sir, that morning."

Bertha and I were married in London, and two weeks afterward we returned to America in the new ship *Glaucus*, commanded by Captain Guy Chesters and his wife.

Our marriage in England instead of America was largely due to the influence of Mary Phillips, who thought it would be much safer and more prudent for us to be married before we again undertook the risks of a sea-voyage.

"Nobody knows what may happen on the ocean," she said; "but if you're once fairly married, that much is accomplished, anyway."

Our choice of a sailing-vessel in which to make the passage was due in a great part to our desire to keep company as long as possible with Captain Chesters and his wife, to whom we truly believed we owed each other.

When we reached New York, and Bertha and I were about to start for the Catskill Mountains, where we proposed to spend the rest of the summer, we took leave of Captain Guy and his wife with warmest expressions of friendship, with plans for meeting again.

Everything seemed to have turned out in the best possible way.

We had each other, and Mary Phillips had some one to manage.

We should have been grieved if we had been obliged to leave her without occupation.

At the moment of parting I drew her aside. "Mary," I said, "we have had some strange experiences together, and I shall never forget them."

"Nor shall I, sir," she answered. "Some of them were so harrowing and close-shaved, and such heart-breaking disappointments I never had. The worst of all was when you threw that rope clean over our ship without holding on to your end of it. I had been dead sure that the rope was going to bring us all together."

"That was a terrible mishap," I answered; "what did Bertha think of it?"

"Bless my soul!" ejaculated Mary Phillips; "she wasn't on deck, and she never knew anything about it. When I am nursing up a love match I don't mention that sort of thing."

# THE BAKER OF BARNBURY.

A CHRISTMAS STORY.

IT was three days before Christmas, and the baker
of the little village of Barnbury sat in the room
behind his shop. He was a short and sturdy baker, a
good fellow, and ordinarily of a jolly demeanor, but
this day he sat grim in his little back room.

"Christmas, indeed," he said to himself, "and what
of Christmas? 'Thank you, baker, and a merry
Christmas to you,' and every one of them goes away
with the present of a raisin-cake, or a horse ginger-
cake, if they like that better. All this for the good
of the trade, of course. Confound the trade, I'm tired
of trade. Is there no good in this world, but the
good of the trade? 'Oh, yes,' they'll say, 'there's
Christmas, and that's good.' — 'But what is the good
of it to me?' say I. Christmas day is a family day,
and to a man without a family it's no day at all. I'm
not even fourth cousin to a soul in the town. Nobody
asks me to a family dinner. 'Bake! baker!' they cry,
'that we may eat and love each other.' Confound
them! I am tired of it. What is Christmas to me?
I have a mind to skip it."

As he said this, a smile broke out on his face.

"Skip Christmas," said he; "that is a good idea. They did not think of me last year; this would make them think of me this year."

As he said this he opened his order-book and ran his eye over the names. "Here's orders from every one of them," said he, "from the doctor down to Cobbler John. All have families, all give orders. It's pastry, cake, or sweetmeats, or it's meat or fowl to be baked. What a jolly Christmas they will have without me! Orders from all of them, every one; all sent in good time for fear of being crowded out."

Here he stopped and ran his eye again over the list.

"No, not all," he said; "the Widow Monk is not here. What is the matter with her, I wonder. The only person in Barnbury who has not ordered either pastry, cakes, or sweetmeats; or fowls or meat to be baked. If I skip Christmas, she'll not mind it, she'll be the only one — the only one in all Barnbury. Ha! ha!"

The baker wanted some fresh air, and, as this was supper-time for the whole village, he locked up his shop and went out for a walk. The night was clear and frosty. He liked this; the air was so different from that in his bakery.

He walked to the end of the village, and at the last house he stopped.

"It's very odd," said he to himself; "no cakes, pastry, or sweetmeats; not even poultry or meat to be baked. I'll look in and see about this," and he knocked at the door.

The Widow Monk was at supper. She was a plump

little body, bright and cheerful to look upon, and not more than thirty.

"Good evening, baker," said she; "will you sit down and have a cup of tea?"

The baker put down his hat, unwound his long woollen comforter, took off his overcoat, and had a cup of tea.

"Now, then," said he to himself, as he put down his cup, "if she'd ask me to dinner, I wouldn't skip Christmas, and the whole village might rise up and bless her."

"We are like to have a fine Christmas," he said to her.

"Fine enough for the rest of you," she said, with a smile, "but I shall not have any Christmas this year."

"How's that?" cried the baker; "no Christmas, Widow Monk?"

"Not this year, baker," said she, and she poured him another cup of tea. "You see that horse-blanket?" said she, pointing to one thrown over a chair.

"Bless me, Widow Monk," cried the baker, "you're not intending to set up a horse?"

"Hardly that," she answered, with a smile, "but that's the very last horse-blanket that I can get to bind. They don't put them on horses, but they have them bound with red, and use them for door curtains. That's all the fashion now, and all the Barnbury folks who can afford them, have sent them to me to be bound with red. That one is nearly finished, and there are no more to be bound."

"But haven't the Barnbury folks any more work for you?" cried the baker; "haven't they shirts or gowns, or some other sort of needling?"

"Those things they make themselves," answered the widow; "but this binding is heavy work, and they give it to me. The blankets are coarse, you see, but they hang well in the doorway."

"Confound the people of Barnbury!" cried the baker. "Every one of them would hang well in a doorway, if I had the doing of it. And so you can't afford a Christmas, Widow Monk?"

"No," said she, setting herself to work on her horse-blanket, "not this year. When I came to Barnbury, baker, I thought I might do well, but I have not done well."

"Did not your husband leave you anything?" he asked.

"My husband was a sailor," said she, "and he went down with his brig, the *Mistletoe*, three years ago, and all that he left me is gone, baker."

It was time for the baker to open his shop, and he went away, and as he walked home snow-drops and tear-drops were all mixed together on his face.

"I couldn't do this sort of thing before her," he said, "and I am glad it was time to go and open my shop."

That night the baker did all his regular work, but not a finger did he put to any Christmas order. The next day, at supper-time, he went out for a walk.

On the way he said to himself, "If she is going to skip Christmas, and I am going to skip Christmas, why should we not skip it together? That would truly be most fit and gladsome, and it would serve Barnbury aright. I'll go in and lay it before her."

The Widow Monk was at supper, and when she asked him to take a cup of tea, he put down his hat, unwound his woollen comforter, and took off his overcoat. When he set down his empty cup he told her that he, too, had made up his mind to skip Christmas, and he told her why, and then he proposed that they should skip it together.

Now, the Widow Monk forgot to ask him to take a second cup of tea, and she turned as red as the binding she had put on the horse-blankets. The baker pushed aside the teacups, leaned over the table, and pressed his suit very hard.

When the time came for him to open his shop she said that she would think about the matter, and that he might come again.

The next day the sun shone golden, the snow shone silvery, and Barnbury was like a paradise to the good baker. For the Widow Monk had told him he might come again, and that was almost the same thing as telling him that he and she would skip Christmas together! And not a finger, so far, had he put to any Christmas order.

About noon of that day, he was so happy, was that good baker, that he went into the village inn to have a taste of something hot. In the inn he found a tall man, with rings in his ears. A sun-browned man he was and a stranger, who had just arrived and wanted

his dinner.   He was also a handsome man, and a
sailor, as any one could see.

As the baker entered, the tall man said to the inn-
keeper : —

"Is there a Mrs. Monk now living in this village?"

"Truly there is," said the inn-keeper, "and I will
show you her house.   But you'll have your dinner
first?"

"Aye, aye," said the stranger, "for I'll not go to
her hungry."

The baker asked for nothing hot, but turned him
and went out into the cold, bleak world.   As he closed
the door behind him he heard the stranger say : —

"On the brig *Mistletoe.*"

It was not needed that the baker should hear these
words; already he knew everything.   His soul had
told him everything in the moment he saw the sun-
browned man with the rings in his ears!

On went the baker, his head bowed on his breast,
the sun shining like tawdry brass, the snow glistening
like a slimy, evil thing.   He knew not where he was
going; he knew not what he intended to do, but on
he went.

Presently a door opened, and he was called.

"I saw you coming," said the Widow Monk, "and
I did not wish to keep you waiting in the cold," and
she held open the door for him.

When he had entered, and had seated himself before the fire, she said to him : —

"Truly, you look chilled ; you need something hot";
and she prepared it for him.

The baker took the hot beverage. This much of good he might at least allow himself. He drank it, and he felt warmed.

"And now," said the Widow Monk, seating herself on the other side of the fire-place, "I shall speak as plainly to you as you spoke to me. You spoke very well yesterday, and I have been thinking about it ever since, and have made up my mind. You are alone in the world, and I am alone; and if you don't wish to be alone any longer, why, I don't wish to be either, and so — perhaps — it will not be necessary to skip Christmas this year."

Alas for the poor baker! Here was paradise seen through a barred gate! But the baker's heart was moved; even in the midst of his misery he could not but be grateful for the widow's words. There flashed into his eyes a sudden brightness. He held out his hands. He would thank her first, and tell her afterwards.

The widow took his hands, lowered her bright eyes and blushed. Then she suddenly withdrew herself and stood up.

"Now," she said, with a pretty smile, "let me do the talking. Don't look so downcast. When I tell you that you have made me very, very happy, you should look happy too. When you came to me yesterday, and said what you said, I thought you were in too much of a hurry; but now I think that perhaps you were right, and that when people of our age have anything important to do, it is well to do it at once; for in this world there are all sorts of things continually springing up to prevent people from being happy."

The whole body of the baker was filled with a great groan, but he denied it utterance. He must hear what she would say.

"And so I was going to suggest," she continued, "that instead of skipping Christmas together, we keep it together. That is all the change I propose to your plan."

Up sprang the baker, so suddenly, that he overset his chair. Now he must speak. The widow stepped quickly toward the door, and, turning with a smile, held up her hand.

"Now, good friend," said she, "stop there! At any moment some one might come in. Hasten back to your shop. At three o'clock I will meet you at the parson's. That will surely be soon enough, even for such a hasty man as you."

The baker came forward, and gasped, "Your husband!"

"Not yet," said the widow, with a laugh, and, kissing the tips of her fingers to him, she closed the door behind her.

Out into the cold went the baker. His head was dazed, but he walked steadfastly to his shop. There was no need for him to go anywhere; to tell anybody anything. The man with the earrings would settle matters for himself soon enough.

The baker put up his shutters and locked his shop door. He would do nothing more for the good of trade; nothing more for the good of anything. Skip

Christmas! Indeed would he! And, moreover, every holiday and every happy day would now be skipped straight on for the rest of his life. He put his house in order; he arranged his affairs; he attired himself in his best apparel; locked his door behind him; and went out into the cold world.

He longed now to get far away from the village. Before the sun set there would not be one soul there who would care for him.

As he hurried on, he saw before him the parson's house.

"I will take but one thing away with me," he said; "I will ask the good old man to give me his blessing. That will I take with me."

"Of course he is in," said the parson's maid; "there, in the parlor."

As the baker entered the parson's parlor, some one hastened to meet him. It was the Widow Monk.

"You wicked man," she whispered, "you are a quarter of an hour late. The parson is waiting."

The parson was a little man with white hair. He stepped toward the couple standing together, and the widow took the baker's hand. Then the parson began the little speech he always made on such occasions. It was full of good sense and very touching, and the widow's eyes were dim with tears. The baker would have spoken, but he had never interrupted a clergyman, and he could not do it now.

Then the parson began his appointed work, and the heart of the baker swelled, as the widow's hand trembled in his own.

"Wilt thou have this woman to be thy wedded wife?" asked the parson.

"Now for this," quoth the poor baker to himself, "I may bake forever, but I cannot draw back nor keep the good man waiting." And he said, "Yes."

Then it was that the baker received what he had come for, — the parson's blessing; and, immediately, his fair companion, brimming with tears, threw herself into his arms.

"Now," said the baker to himself, "when I leave this house, may the devil take me, and right welcome shall he be!"

"Dearest," she exclaimed, as she looked into his face, "you cannot know how happy I am. My wedding day, and my brother back from the cruel seas!"

Struck by a sudden blast of bewildering ecstasy, the baker raised his eyes, and beheld the tall form of the sun-browned stranger who had been standing behind them.

"You are not a sailor-man," quoth the jovial brother, "like my old mate, who went down in the brig *Mistletoe,* but my sister tells me you are a jolly good fellow, and I wish you fair winds and paying cargoes." And after giving the baker a powerful handshake, the sailor kissed the bride, the parson's wife, the parson's daughter, and the parson's maid, and wished the family were larger, having just returned from the cruel seas.

The only people in the village of Barnbury, who thoroughly enjoyed the Christmas of that year, were the baker, his wife, and the sailor brother. And a rare good time they had; for a big sea-chest arrived, and there were curious presents, and a tall flask of rare old wine, and plenty of time for three merry people to cook for themselves.

The baker told his wife of his soul-harrowing plight of the day before.

"Now, then," said he, "don't you think that by rights I should bake all the same?"

"Oh, that will be skipped," she said, with a laugh; "and now go you and make ready for the cakes, pastry, and sweetmeats, the baked meats and the poultry, with which the people of Barnbury are to be made right happy on New Year's day."

# THE WATER-DEVIL.

## A MARINE TALE.

IN the village of Riprock there was neither tavern
nor inn, for it was but a small place through which
few travellers passed; but it could not be said to be
without a place of entertainment, for if by chance a
stranger — or two or three of them, for that matter —
wished to stop at Riprock for a meal, or to pass the
night, there was the house of blacksmith Fryker,
which was understood to be always open to decent
travellers.

The blacksmith was a prominent man in the village,
and his house was a large one, with several spare bed-
rooms, and it was said by those who had had an opportunity of judging, that nobody in the village lived
better than blacksmith Fryker and his family.

Into the village there came, late one autumn afternoon, a tall man, who was travelling on foot, with a
small valise hanging from his shoulder. He had inquired for lodging for the night, had been directed to
the blacksmith's house, had arranged to stop there,
had had his supper, which greatly satisfied him, and
was now sitting before the fire in the large living-
room, smoking blacksmith Fryker's biggest pipe.

This stranger was a red-haired man, with a cheery expression, and a pair of quick, bright eyes. He was slenderly but strongly built, and was a good fellow, who would stand by, with his hands in the pockets of his short pea-jacket, and right willingly tell one who was doing something how the thing ought to be done.

But the traveller did not sit alone before the crackling fire of logs, for the night being cool, a table was drawn near to one side of the fire-place, and by this sat Mistress Fryker and her daughter Joanna, both engaged in some sort of needle-work. The blacksmith sat between the corner of the fire-place and this table, so that when he had finished smoking his after-supper pipe, he might put on his spectacles and read the weekly paper by the light of the big lamp. On the other side of the stranger, whose chair was in front of the middle of the fire-place, sat the school-master, Andrew Cardly by name; a middle-aged man of sober and attentive aspect, and very glad when chance threw in his way a book he had not read, or a stranger who could reinforce his stock of information. At the other corner of the fire-place, in a cushioned chair, which was always given to him when he dropped in to spend an evening with the blacksmith, sat Mr. Harberry, an elderly man, a man of substance, and a man in whom all Riprock, not excluding himself, placed unqualified confidence as to his veracity, his financial soundness, and his deep insight into the causes, the influences, and the final issue of events and conditions.

"On a night like this," said the stranger, stretching his long legs toward the blaze, "there is nothing I like better than a fire of wood, except indeed it be the society of ladies who do not object to a little tobacco smoke," and he glanced with a smile toward the table with a lamp upon it.

Now blacksmith Fryker was a prudent man, and he did not consider that the privileges of his hearthstone — always freely granted to a decent stranger — included an acquaintance with his pretty daughter; and so, without allowing his women-folk a chance to enter into the conversation, he offered the stranger a different subject to hammer upon.

"In the lower country," said he, "they don't need fires as early in the season as we do. What calling do you follow, sir? Some kind of trade, perhaps?"

"No," said the traveller, "I follow no trade; I follow the sea."

At this the three men looked at him, as also the two women. His appearance no more suggested that he was a seaman than the appearance of Mr. Harberry suggested that he was what the village of Riprock believed him to be.

"I should not have taken you for a sailor," said the blacksmith.

"I am not a sailor," said the other; "I am a soldier; a sea-soldier — in fact, a marine."

"I should say, sir," remarked the school-master, in a manner intended rather to draw out information than to give it, "that the position of a soldier on a ship possessed advantages over that of a soldier on land. The former is not required to make long marches, nor to carry heavy baggage. He remains at rest, in fact, while traversing great distances. Nor is he called on to resist the charges of cavalry, nor to form hollow squares on the deadly battle-field."

The stranger smiled. "We often find it hard enough," said he, "to resist the charges made against us by our officers; the hollow squares form themselves in our stomachs when we are on short rations; and I have known many a man who would rather walk twenty miles than sail one, especially when the sea chops."

"I am very sure, sir," said school-master Cardly, "that there is nothing to be said against the endurance and the courage of marines. We all remember how they presented arms, and went down with the *Royal George.*"

The marine smiled.

"I suppose," said the blacksmith, "that you never had to do anything of that sort?"

The stranger did not immediately answer, but sat looking into the fire. Presently he said: "I have done things of nearly every sort, although not exactly that; but I have thought my ship was going down with all on board, and that's the next worst thing to going down, you know."

"And how was that?" inquired Fryker.

"Well," said the other, "it happened more times than I can tell you of, or even remember. Yes," said he, meditatively, "more times than I can remember."

"I am sure," said the school-master, "that we should all like to hear some of your experiences."

The marine shrugged his shoulders. "These

things," said he, "come to a man, and then if he lives through them, they pass on, and he is ready for the next streak of luck, good or bad. That's the way with us followers of the sea, especially if we happen to be marines, and have to bear, so to speak, the responsibility of two professions. But sometimes a mischance or a disaster does fix itself upon a man's mind so that he can tell about it if he is called upon; and just now there comes to my mind a very odd thing which once happened to. me, and I can give you the points of that, if you like."

The three men assured him that they would very much like it, and the two women looked as if they were of the same opinion.

Before he began the marine glanced about him, with a certain good-natured wistfulness which might have indicated, to those who understood the countenances of the sea-going classes, a desire to wet his whistle; but if this expression were so intended it was thrown away, for blacksmith Fryker took no spirits himself, nor furnished them to anybody else. Giving up all hope in this direction, the marine took a long pull at his pipe and began.

"It was in the winter of 1878 that I was on the Bay of Bengal, on my way to Calcutta, and about five hundred miles distant from that city. I was not on my own ship, but was returning from a leave of absence on an American steamer from San Francisco to Calcutta, where my vessel, the United States frigate *Apache*, was then lying. My leave of absence would expire in three days; but although the *General Brooks*, the vessel I was aboard of, was more of a freight than a passenger vessel, and was heavily laden, we would have been in port in good time if, two days before, something had not happened to the machinery. I am not a machinist myself, and don't know exactly what it was that was out of order, but the engine stopped, and we had to proceed under sail. That sounds like a slow business; but the *Brooks* was a clipper-built vessel with three masts and a lot of sails — square sails, fore-and-aft sails, jib sails, and all that sort of thing. I am not a regular sailor myself, and don't know the names of all the sails; but whatever sails she could have she did have, and although she was an iron vessel, and heavily freighted, she was a good sailer. We had a strong, steady wind from the south, and the captain told me that at the rate we were going he didn't doubt that he would get me aboard my vessel before my leave ran out, or at least so soon afterward that it wouldn't make any difference.

"Well, as I said, the wind blew strong and steady behind us, the sails were full, and the spray dashed up at our bow in a way calculated to tickle the soul of any one anxious to get to the end of his voyage; and I was one of that sort, I can tell you.

"In the afternoon of the second day after our engine stopped, I was standing at the bow, and looking over, when suddenly I noticed that there wasn't any spray dashing up in front of the vessel. I thought we must have struck a sudden calm, but, glancing up, I saw the sails were full, and the wind blew fair in my face as I turned toward the stern. I walked aft to the skipper, and touching my cap, I said, 'Captain, how is it that when a ship is dashing along at this rate she doesn't throw up any spray with her cutwater?' He grinned a little, and said, 'But she does, you know.' 'If you will come forward,' said I, 'I'll show you that she doesn't,' and then we walked forward, and I showed him that she didn't. I never saw a man so surprised. At first he thought that somebody had been squirting oil in front, but even if that had been the case, there would have been some sort of a ripple on each side of the bow, and there wasn't anything of the kind. The skipper took off his cap and scratched his head. Then he turned and sang out, 'Mr. Rogers, throw the log.'

"Now the log," said the marine, turning to Mrs. Fryker and her daughter, "is a little piece of wood with a long line to it, that they throw out behind a vessel to see how fast she is going. I am not a regular Jack Tar myself, and don't understand the principle of the thing, but it tells you exactly how many miles an hour the ship is going.

"In about two minutes Mr. Rogers stepped up, with his eyes like two auger-holes, and said he, 'Captain, we're makin' no knots an hour. We're not sailing at all.'

"'Get out,' roared the captain, 'don't you see the sails? Don't you feel the wind? Throw that log again, sir.'

"Well, they threw the log again, the captain saw it done, and sure enough Mr. Rogers was right. The vessel wasn't moving. With a wind that ought to have carried her spinning along, miles and miles in an hour, she was standing stock-still. The skipper here let out one of the strongest imprecations used in navigation, and said he, 'Mr. Rogers, is it possible that there is a sand-bar in the middle of the Bay of Bengal, and that we've stuck on it ? Cast the lead.'

"I will just state to the ladies," said the marine, turning toward the table, "that the lead is a heavy weight that is lowered to the bottom of a body of water to see how deep it is, and this operation is called sounding. Well, they sounded and they sounded, but everywhere — fore, aft, and midship — they found plenty of water; in fact, not having a line for deep-sea sounding they couldn't touch bottom at all.

"I can tell you, ladies and gentlemen," said the marine, looking from one to the other of the party, "that things now began to feel creepy. I am not afraid of storms, nor fires at sea, nor any of the common accidents of the ocean; but for a ship to stand still with plenty of water under her, and a strong wind filling her sails, has more of the uncanny about it than I fancy. Pretty near the whole of the crew was on deck by this time, and I could see that they felt very much as I did, but nobody seemed to know what to say about it.

" Suddenly the captain thought that some unknown current was setting against us, and forcing the vessel back with the same power that the wind was forcing her forward, and he tried to put the ship about so as to have the wind on her starboard quarter ; but as she hadn't any headway, or for some other reason, this didn't work. Then it struck him that perhaps one of the anchors had been accidentally dropped, but they were all in their places, and if one of them had dropped, its cable would not have been long enough to touch bottom.

"Now I could see that he began to look scared. 'Mr. Browser,' said he, to the chief engineer, 'for some reason or other this ship does not make headway under sail. You must go to work and get the engine running.' And for the rest of that day everybody on board who understood that sort of thing was down below, hard at work with the machinery, hammering and banging like good fellows.

"The chief officer ordered a good many of the sails to be taken in, for they were only uselessly straining the masts, but there were enough left to move her in case the power of the current, or whatever it was that stopped her, had slackened, and she steadily kept her position with the breeze abaft.

"All the crew, who were not working below, were crowded together on deck, talking about this strange thing. I joined them, and soon found that they thought it was useless to waste time and labor on the machinery. They didn't believe it could be mended, and if it should be, how could an engine move a vessel that the wind couldn't stir?

"These men were of many nationalities — Dutch, Scandinavian, Spanish, Italian, South American, and a lot more. Like many other American vessels that sail from our ports, nearly all the officers and crew were foreigners. The captain was a Finlander, who spoke very good English. And the only man who called himself an American was the chief officer; and he was only half a one; for he was born in Germany, came to the United States when he was twenty years old, stayed there five years, which didn't count either way, and had now been naturalized for twenty years.

"The consequence of this variety in nationality was that the men had all sorts of ideas and notions regarding the thing that was happening. They had thrown over chips and bits of paper to see if the vessel had begun to move, and had found that she didn't budge an inch, and now they seemed afraid to look over the sides.

"They were a superstitious lot, as might be expected, and they all believed that, in some way or other, the ship was bewitched; and in fact I felt like agreeing with them, although I did not say so.

"There was an old Portuguese sailor on board, an ugly-looking, weather-beaten little fellow, and when he had listened to everything the others had to say, he shuffled himself into the middle of the group. 'Look here, mates,' said he, in good enough English, 'it's no use talking no more about this. I know what's the matter; I've sailed these seas afore, and I've been along the coast of this bay all the way from Negapatam to Jellasore on the west coast, and from Chittagong to Kraw on the other; and I have heard stories of the strange things that are in this Bay of Bengal, and what they do, and the worst of them all is the Water-devil — and he's got us!'

"When the old rascal said this, there wasn't a man on deck who didn't look pale, in spite of his dirt and his sunburn. The chief officer tried to keep his knees stiff, but I could see him shaking. 'What's a Water-devil?' said he, trying to make believe he thought it all stuff and nonsense. The Portuguese touched his forelock. 'Do you remember, sir,' said he, 'what was the latitude and longitude when you took your observation to-day?' 'Yes,' said the other, 'it was 15° north and 90° east.' The Portuguese nodded his head. 'That's just about the spot, sir, just about. I can't say exactly where the spot is, but it's just about here, and we've struck it. There isn't a native seaman on any of these coasts that would sail over that point if he knowed it and could help it, for that's the spot where the Water-devil lives.'

"It made me jump to hear the grunt that went through that crowd when he said this, but nobody asked any questions, and he went on. 'This here Water-devil,' said he, 'is about as big as six whales, and in shape very like an oyster without its shell, and he fastens himself to the rocks at the bottom with a million claws. Right out of the middle of him there grows up a long arm that reaches to the top of the water, and at the end of this arm is a fist about the size of a yawl-boat, with fifty-two fingers to it, with each one of them covered with little suckers that will stick fast to anything — iron, wood, stone, or flesh. All that this Water-devil gets to eat is what happens to come swimmin' or sailin' along where he can reach it, and it doesn't matter to him whether it's a shark, or a porpoise, or a shipful of people, and when he takes a grab of anything, that thing never gets away.'

"About this time there were five or six men on their knees saying their prayers, such as they were, and a good many others looked as if they were just about to drop.

"'Now, when this Water-devil gets hold of a ship,' the old fellow went on, 'he don't generally pull her straight down to the bottom, but holds on to it till he counts his claws, and sees that they are all fastened to the rocks; for if a good many of them wasn't fastened he might pull himself loose, instead of pulling the ship down, and then he'd be a goner, for he'd be towed away, and like as not put in a museum. But when he is satisfied that he is moored fast and strong, then he hauls on his arm, and down comes the ship, no matter how big she is. As the ship is sinkin' he turns her over, every now and then, keel uppermost, and gives her a shake, and when the people drop out, he sucks them into a sort of funnel, which is his mouth.'

"'Does he count fast?' asked one of the men, this being the first question that had been asked.

"'I've heard,' said the Portuguese, 'that he's a rapid calculator, and the minute he's got to his millionth claw, and finds it's hooked tight and fast, he begins to haul down the ship.'"

At this point the marine stopped and glanced around at the little group. The blacksmith's wife and daughter had put down their work, and were gazing at him with an air of horrified curiosity. The blacksmith held his pipe in his hand, and regarded the narrator with the steadiness and impassiveness of an anvil. The school-master was listening with the greatest eagerness. He was an enthusiast on Natural History and Mythology, and had written an article for a weekly paper on the reconciliation of the beasts of tradition with the fauna of to-day. Mr. Harberry was not looking at the marine. His eyes were fixed upon the school-master.

"Mr. Cardly," said he, "did you ever read of an animal like that?"

"I cannot say that I have," was his reply; "but it is certain that there are many strange creatures, especially in the sea, of which scientists are comparatively ignorant."

"Such as the sea-serpent," added the marine, quickly, "and a great many other monsters who are not in the books, but who have a good time at the bottom of the sea, all the same. Well, to go on with my story, you must understand that, though this Portuguese spoke broken English, which I haven't tried to give you, he made himself perfectly plain to all of us, and I can assure you that when he got through talking there was a shaky lot of men on that deck.

"The chief officer said he would go below and see how the captain was getting on, and the crew huddled together in the bow, and began whispering among themselves, as if they were afraid the Water-devil would hear them. I turned to walk aft, feeling pretty queer, I can tell you, when I saw Miss Minturn just coming up from the cabin below.

"I haven't said anything about Miss Minturn, but she and her father, who was an elderly English gentleman and an invalid, who had never left his berth since we took him up at Singapore, were our only passengers, except, of course, myself. She was a beautiful girl, with soft blue eyes and golden hair, and a little pale from constantly staying below to nurse her father.

"Of course I had had little or nothing to say to her, for her father was a good deal of a swell and I was only a marine; but now she saw me standing there by myself, and she came right up to me. 'Can you tell me, sir,' she said, 'if anything else has happened? They are making a great din in the engine-room. I have been looking out of our port, and the vessel seems to me to be stationary.' She stopped at that, and waited to hear what I had to say, but I assure you I would have liked to have had her go on talking for half an hour. Her voice was rich and sweet, like that of so many Englishwomen, although, I am happy to say, a great many of my countrywomen have just as good voices; and when I meet any of them for the first time, I generally give them the credit of talking in soft and musical notes, even though I have not had the pleasure of hearing them speak."

"Look here," said the blacksmith, "can't you skip the girl and get back to the Devil?"

"No," said the marine, "I couldn't do that. The two are mixed together, so to speak, so that I have to tell you of both of them."

"You don't mean to say," exclaimed Mrs. Fryker, speaking for the first time, and by no means in soft and musical tones, "that he swallowed her?"

"I'll go on with the story," said the marine; "that's the best way, and everything will come up in its place. Now, of course, I wasn't going to tell this charming young woman, with a sick father, anything about the Water-devil, though what reason to give her for our standing still here I couldn't imagine; but of course I had to speak, and I said, 'Don't be alarmed, miss, we have met with an unavoidable detention; that sort of thing often happens in navigation. I can't explain it to you, but you see the ship is perfectly safe and sound, and she is merely under sail instead of having her engines going.'

"'I understood about that,' said she, 'and father and I were both perfectly satisfied; for he said that if we had a good breeze we would not be long in reaching Calcutta; but we seem to have a breeze, and yet we don't go.' 'You'll notice,' said I, 'that the sails are not all set, and for some reason the wind does not serve. When the engines are mended, we shall probably go spinning along.' She looked as if she was trying to appear satisfied. 'Thank you, sir,' she said. 'I hope we may shortly proceed on our way, but in the meantime I shall not say anything to my father about this detention. I think he has not noticed it.' 'That would be very wise,' I replied, and as she turned toward the companionway I was wild to say to her that it would be a lot better for her to stay on deck, and get some good fresh air, instead of cooping herself up in that close cabin; but I didn't know her well enough for that."

"Now that you are through with the girl," said the blacksmith, "what did the Devil do?"

"I haven't got to him yet," said the marine, "but after Miss Minturn went below I began to think of him, and the more I thought of him, the less I liked him. I think the chief officer must have told the men below about the Water-devil, for pretty soon the whole kit and boodle of them left their work and came on deck, skipper and all. They told me they had given up the engine as a bad job, and I thought to myself that most likely they were all too nervous to rightly know what they were about. The captain threw out the log again, but it floated alongside like a cork on a fishing-line, and at this he turned pale and walked away from the ship's side, forgetting to pull it in again.

"It was now beginning to grow dark, and as nobody seemed to think about supper, I went below to look into that matter. It wouldn't do for Miss Minturn and her father to go without their regular meal, for that would be sure to scare them to death; and if I'm to have a big scare I like to take it on a good square meal, so I went below to see about it. But I wasn't needed, for Miss Minturn's maid, who was an elderly woman, and pretty sharp set in her temper, was in the cook's galley superintending supper for her people, and after she got through I superintended some for myself.

"After that I felt a good deal bolder, and I lighted

a pipe and went on deck. There I found the whole ship's company, officers and crew, none of them doing anything, and most of them clustered together in little groups, whispering or grunting.

"I went up to the captain and asked him what he was going to do next. 'Do?' said he; 'there is nothing to do; I've done everything that I can do. I'm all upset; I don't know whether I am myself or some other man'; and then he walked away.

"I sat there and smoked and looked at them, and I can tell you the sight wasn't cheerful. There was the ship, just as good and sound, as far as anybody could see, as anything that floated on the ocean, and here were all her people, shivering and shaking and not speaking above their breath, looking for all the world, under the light of the stars and the ship's lamps, which some of them had had sense enough to light, as if they expected in the course of the next half-hour, to be made to walk the plank; and, to tell the truth, what they were afraid of would come to pretty much the same thing."

"Mr. Cardly," here interrupted Mr. Harberry, "how long does it take to count a million?"

"That depends," said the school-master, "on the rapidity of the calculator; some calculators count faster than others. An ordinary boy, counting two hundred a minute, would require nearly three days and a half to count a million."

"Very good," said Mr. Harberry; "please go on with your story, sir."

"Of course," said the marine, "there is a great difference between a boy and a Water-devil, and it is impossible for anybody to know how fast the latter can count, especially as he may be supposed to be used to it. Well, I couldn't stand it any longer on deck, and having nothing else to do, I turned in and went to sleep."

"To sleep! Went to sleep!" exclaimed Mrs. Fryker. "I don't see how you could have done that."

"Ah, madam," said the marine, "we soldiers of the sea are exposed to all sorts of dangers,—combination dangers, you might call them,—and in the course of time we get used to it; if we didn't we couldn't do our duty.

"As the ship had been in its present predicament for six or seven hours, and nothing had happened, there was no reason to suppose that things would not remain as they were for six or seven hours more, in which time I might get a good sleep, and be better prepared for what might come. There's nothing like a good meal and a good sleep as a preparation for danger.

"It was daylight when I awakened, and rapidly glancing about me, I saw that everything appeared to be all right. Looking out of the port-hole, I could see that the vessel was still motionless. I hurried on deck, and was greatly surprised to find nobody there —no one on watch, no one at the wheel, no one anywhere. I ran down into the fo'castle, which is the sailors' quarters, but not a soul could I see. I called, I whistled, I searched everywhere, but no one answered; I could find no one. Then I dashed up on deck, and glared around me. Every boat was gone.

"Now I knew what had happened: the cowardly rascals, from captain to cook, had deserted the ship in the night, and I had been left behind!

"For some minutes I stood motionless, wondering how men could be so unfeeling as to do such a thing. I soon became convinced, from what I had seen of the crew, that they had not all gone off together, that there had been no concerted action. A number of them had probably quietly lowered a boat and sneaked away; then another lot had gone off, hoping their mates would not hear them and therefore crowd into their boat. And so they had all departed, not one boat-load thinking of anybody but themselves; or if they thought at all about others, quieting their consciences by supposing that there were enough boats on the vessel, and that the other people were as likely to get off as they were.

"Suddenly I thought of the other passengers. Had they been left behind? I ran down below, and I had scarcely reached the bottom of the steps when I met Miss Minturn's maid. 'It seems to me,' she said, sharply, 'that the people on this ship are neglecting their duty. There's nobody in the kitchen, and I want some gruel.' 'My good woman,' said I, 'who do you want it for?' 'Who!' she replied; 'why, for Mr. Minturn, of course; and Miss Minturn may like some, too.'

"Then I knew that all the passengers had been left behind!

"'If you want any gruel,' said I, 'you will have to go into the galley and make it yourself'; and then in

a low tone I told her what had happened, for I knew
that it would be much better for me to do this than
for her to find it out for herself. Without a word she
sat right down on the floor, and covered her head with
her apron. 'Now don't make a row,' said I, 'and
frighten your master and mistress to death; we're all
right so far, and all you've got to do is to take care of
Mr. and Miss Minturn, and cook their meals. The
steamer is tight and sound, and it can't be long before some sort of a craft will come by and take us off.'
I left her sniffling with her apron over her head, but
when I came back, ten minutes afterward, she was in
the galley making gruel.

"I don't think you will be surprised, my friends,"
continued the marine, "when I tell you that I now
found myself in a terrible state of mind. Of course I
hadn't felt very jovial since the steamer had been so
wonderfully stopped; but when the captain and all
the crew were aboard, I had that sort of confidence
which comes from believing that when there are people about whose duty it is to do things, when the time
comes to do the things, they will do them; but now,
practically speaking, there was nobody but me. The
others on board were not to be counted, except as en-
cumbrances. In truth, I was alone, — alone with the
Water-devil!

"The moment I found no one to depend upon but
myself, and that I was deserted in the midst of this
lonely mass of water, in that moment did my belief
in the Water-devil begin to grow. When I first heard
of the creature, I didn't consider that it was my busi-

ness either to believe in it, or not to believe in it, and
I could let the whole thing drop out of my mind, if
I chose; but now it was a different matter. I was
bound to think for myself, and the more I thought,
the more I believed in the Water-devil.

"The fact was, there wasn't anything else to believe
in. I had gone over the whole question, and the skipper had gone all over it, and everybody else had gone
all over it, and no one could think of anything but a
Water-devil that could stop a steamer in this way in
the middle of the Bay of Bengal, and hold her there
hour after hour, in spite of wind and wave and tide.
It could not be anything but the monster the Portuguese had told us of, and all I now could do was to
wonder whether, when he was done counting his million claws, he would be able to pull down a vessel of
a thousand tons, for that was about the size of the
*General Brooks.*

"I think I should now have begun to lose my wits
if it had not been for one thing, and that was the
coming of Miss Minturn on deck. The moment I saw
her lovely face I stiffened up wonderfully. 'Sir,' said
she, 'I would like to see the captain.' 'I am repre-
senting the captain, miss,' I said, with a bow; 'what
is it that I can do for you?' 'I want to speak to him
about the steward,' she said; 'I think he is neglecting his duty.' 'I also represent the steward,' I
replied; 'tell me what you wish of him.' She made
no answer to this, but looked about her in a startled
way. 'Where are all the men?' she said. 'Miss
Minturn,' said I, 'I represent the crew — in fact, I

represent the whole ship's company except the cook, and his place must be taken by your maid.' 'What do you mean?' she asked, looking at me with her wide-opened, beautiful eyes.

"Then, as there was no help for it, I told her everything, except that I did not mention the Water-devil in connection with our marvellous stoppage. I only said that that was caused by something which nobody understood.

"She did not sit down and cover her head, nor did she scream or faint. She turned pale, but looked steadily at me, and her voice did not shake as she asked me what was to be done. 'There is nothing to be done,' I answered, 'but to keep up good hearts, eat three meals a day, and wait until a ship comes along and takes us off.'

"She stood silent for about three minutes. 'I think,' she then said, 'that I will not yet tell my father what has happened'; and she went below.

"Now, strange to say, I walked up and down the deck with my hat cocked on one side and my hands in my pockets, feeling a great deal better. I did not like Water-devils any more than I did before, and I did not believe in this one any less than I did before, but, after all, there was some good about him. It seems odd, but the arm of this submarine monster, over a mile long for all that I knew, was a bond of union between the lovely Miss Minturn and me. She was a lady; I was a marine. So far as I knew anything about bonds of union, there wasn't one that could have tackled itself to us two, except this long, slippery arm of the Water-devil, with one end in the monstrous flob at the bottom, and the other fast to our ship.

"There was no doubt about it, if it hadn't been for that Water-devil she would have been no more to me than the Queen of Madagascar was; but under the circumstances, if I wasn't everything to her, who could be anything — that is, if one looked at the matter from a practical point of view?"

The blacksmith made a little movement of impatience. "Suppose you cut all that," said he. "I don't care about the bond of union; I want to know what happened to the ship."

"It is likely," said the marine, "if I could have cut the bond of union that I spoke of, that is to say, the Water-devil's arm, that I would have done it, hoping that I might safely float off somewhere with Miss Minturn; but I couldn't cut it then, and I can't cut it now. That bond is part of my story, and it must all go on together.

"I now set myself to work to do what I thought ought to be done under the circumstances, but, of course, that wasn't very much. I hoisted a flag upside down, and after considering the matter I concluded to take in all the sails that had been set. I thought that a steamer without smoke coming from her funnel, and no sails set, would be more likely to attract attention from distant vessels than if she appeared to be under sail.

"I am not a regular sailor, as I said before, but I got out on the yard, and cut the square sail loose and let it drop on the deck, and I let the jib come down on a run, and managed to bundle it up some way on the bowsprit. This sort of thing took all the nautical gymnastics that I was master of, and entirely occupied my mind, so that I found myself whistling while I worked. I hoped Miss Minturn heard me whistle, because it would not only give her courage, but would let her see that I was not a man who couldn't keep up his spirits in a case like this.

"When that work was over, I began to wonder what I should do next, and then an idea struck me. 'Suppose,' thought I, 'that we are not stationary, but that we are in some queer kind of a current, and that the water, ship and all are steadily moving on together, so that after awhile we shall come in sight of land, or into the track of vessels!'

"I instantly set about to find out if this was the case. It was about noon, and it so happened that on the day before, when the chief officer took his observation, I was seized with a desire to watch him and see how he did it. I don't see why I should have had this notion, but I had it, and I paid the strictest attention to the whole business, calculation part and all, and I found out exactly how it was done.

"Well, then, I went and got the quadrant, — that's the thing they do it with, — and I took an observation, and I found that we were in latitude 15° north, 90° east, exactly where we had been twenty-four hours before!

"When I found out this, I turned so faint that I wanted to sit down and cover up my head. The Water-devil had us, there was no mistake about it, and no use trying to think of anything else. I staggered along the deck, went below, and cooked myself a meal. In a case like this there's nothing like a square meal to keep a man up.

"I know you don't like to hear her mentioned," said the marine, turning to the blacksmith, "but I am bound to say that in course of the afternoon Miss Minturn came on deck several times, to ask if anything new had happened, and if I had seen a vessel. I showed her all that I had done, and told her I was going to hang out lights at night, and did everything I could to keep her on deck as long as possible; for it was easy to see that she needed fresh air, and I needed company. As long as I was talking to her I didn't care a snap of my finger for the Water-devil. It is queer what an influence a beautiful woman has on a man, but it's so, and there's no use arguing about it. She said she had been puzzling her brains to find out what had stopped us, and she supposed it must be that we had run onto a shallow place and stuck fast in the mud, but thought it wonderful that there should be such a place so far from land. I agreed with her that it was wonderful, and added that that was probably the reason the captain and the crew had been seized with a panic. But sensible people like herself and her father, I said, ought not to be troubled by such an occurrence, especially as the vessel remained in a perfectly sound condition.

"She said that her father was busily engaged in writing his memoirs, and that his mind was so occupied, he had not concerned himself at all about our situation, that is, if he had noticed that we were not moving. 'If he wants to see the steward, or anybody else,' I said, 'please call upon me. You know I represent the whole ship's company, and I shall be delighted to do anything for him or for you.' She thanked me very much and went below.

"She came up again, after this, but her maid came with her, and the two walked on deck for a while. I didn't have much to say to them that time; but just before dark Miss Minturn came on deck alone, and walked forward, where I happened to be. 'Sir,' said she, and her voice trembled a little as she spoke, 'if anything should happen, will you promise me that you will try to save my father?' You can't imagine how these touching words from this beautiful woman affected me. 'My dear lady,' said I, and I hope she did not take offence at the warmth of my expression, 'I don't see how anything can happen; but I promise you, on the word of a sea-soldier, that if danger should come upon us, I will save not only your father, but yourself and your maid. Trust me for that.'

"The look she gave me when I said these words, and especially the flash of her eye when I spoke of my being a sea-soldier, made me feel strong enough to tear that sea-monster's arm in twain, and to sail away with the lovely creature for whom my heart was beginning to throb."

"It's a pity," said the blacksmith, "that you hadn't jumped into the water while the fit was on you, and done the tearing."

"A man often feels strong enough to do a thing,"

said the marine, "and yet doesn't care to try to do it,
and that was my case at that time; but I vowed to
myself that if the time came when there was any
saving to be done, I'd attend to Miss Minturn, even
if I had to neglect the rest of the family.

"She didn't make any answer, but she gave me her
hand; and she couldn't have done anything I liked
better than that. I held it as long as I could, which
wasn't very long, and then she went down to her
father."

"Glad of it," said the blacksmith.

"When I had had my supper, and had smoked my
pipe, and everything was still, and I knew I shouldn't
see anybody any more that night, I began to have the
quakes and the shakes. If even I had had the maid
to talk to, it would have been a comfort; but in the
way of faithfully attending to her employers that
woman was a trump. She cooked for them, and did
for them, and stuck by them straight along, so she
hadn't any time for chats with me.

"Being alone, I couldn't help all the time thinking
about the Water-devil, and although it seems a foolish
thing now that I look back on it, I set to work to
calculate how long it would take him to count his
feet. I made it about the same time as you did, sir,"
nodding to the school-master, "only I considered that
if he counted twelve hours, and slept and rested
twelve hours, that would make it seven days, which
would give me a good long time with Miss Minturn,
and that would be the greatest of joys to me, no
matter what happened afterward.

"But then nobody could be certain that the monster at the bottom of the bay needed rest or sleep. He might be able to count without stopping, and how did I know that he couldn't check off four hundred claws a minute? If that happened to be the case, our time must be nearly up.

"When that idea came into my head, I jumped up and began to walk about. What could I do? I certainly ought to be ready to do something when the time came. I thought of getting life-preservers, and strapping one on each of us, so that if the Water-devil turned over the vessel and shook us out, we shouldn't sink down to him, but would float on the surface.

"But then the thought struck me that if he should find the vessel empty of live creatures, and should see us floating around on the top, all he had to do was to let go of the ship and grab us, one at a time. When I thought of a fist as big as a yawl-boat, clapping its fifty-two fingers on me, it sent a shiver through my bones. The fact was there wasn't anything to do, and so after a while I managed to get asleep, which was a great comfort."

"Mr. Cardly," said Mr. Harberry to the schoolmaster, "what reason can you assign why a sea-monster, such as has been described to us, should neglect to seize upon several small boats filled with men who were escaping from a vessel which it held in custody?"

"I do not precisely see," answered Mr. Cardly, "why these men should have been allowed this immunity, but I —"

"Oh, that is easily explained," interrupted the marine, "for of course the Water-devil could not know that a lot more people were not left in the ship, and if he let go his hold on her, to try and grab a boat that was moving as fast as men could row it, the steamer might get out of his reach, and he mightn't have another chance for a hundred years to make fast to a vessel. No, sir, a creature like that isn't apt to take any wild chances, when he's got hold of a really good thing. Anyway, we were held tight and fast, for at twelve o'clock the next day I took another observation, and there we were, in the same latitude and longitude that we had been in for two days. I took the captain's glass, and I looked all over the water of that bay, which, as I think I have said before, was all the same as the ocean, being somewhere about a thousand miles wide. Not a sail, not a puff of smoke could I see. It must have been a slack season for navigation, or else we were out of the common track of vessels; I had never known that the Bay of Bengal was so desperately lonely.

"It seems unnatural, and I can hardly believe it, when I look back on it, but it's a fact, that I was beginning to get used to the situation. We had plenty to eat, the weather was fine — in fact, there was now only breeze enough to make things cool and comfortable. I was head-man on that vessel, and Miss Minturn might come on deck at any moment, and as long as I could forget that there was a Water-devil fastened to the bottom of the vessel, there was no reason why I should not be perfectly satisfied with

things as they were. And if things had stayed as
they were, for two or three months, I should have
been right well pleased, especially since Miss Minturn's maid, by order of her mistress, had begun to
cook my meals, which she did in a manner truly first-
class. I believed then, and I stand to it now, that
there is no better proof of a woman's good feeling
toward a man, than for her to show an interest in his
meals. That's the sort of sympathy that comes home
to a man, and tells on him, body and soul."

As the marine made this remark, he glanced at the
blacksmith's daughter; but that young lady had taken
up her sewing and appeared to be giving it her earnest
attention. He then went on with his story.

"But things did not remain as they were. The
next morning, about half an hour after breakfast, I
was walking up and down the upper deck, smoking
my pipe, and wondering when Miss Minturn would be
coming up to talk to me about the state of affairs,
when suddenly I felt the deck beneath me move with
a quick, sharp jerk, something like, I imagine, a small
shock of an earthquake.

"Never, in all my life, did the blood run so cold in
my veins; my legs trembled so that I could scarcely
stand. I knew what had happened, — the Water-devil
had begun to haul upon the ship!

"I was in such a state of collapse that I did not
seem to have any power over my muscles; but for all
that, I heard Miss Minturn's voice at the foot of the
companion-way, and knew that she was coming on
deck. In spite of the dreadful awfulness of that mo-

ment, I felt it would never do for her to see me in the
condition I was in, and so, shuffling and half-tumbling,
I got forward, went below, and made my way to the
steward's room, where I had already discovered some
spirits, and I took a good dram; for although I am
not by any means an habitual drinker, being princi-
pled against that sort of thing, there are times when
a man needs the support of some good brandy or
whiskey.

"In a few minutes I felt more like myself, and
went on deck, and there was Miss Minturn, half-
scared to death. 'What is the meaning of that
shock?' she said; 'have we struck anything?' 'My
dear lady,' said I, with as cheerful a front as I could
put on, 'I do not think we have struck anything.
There is nothing to strike.' She looked at me for a
moment like an angel ready to cry, and clasping her
hands, she said, 'Oh, tell me, sir, I pray you, sir, tell
me what has happened. My father felt that shock.
He sent me to inquire about it. His mind is disturbed.' At that moment, before I could make an
answer, there was another jerk of the ship, and we
both went down on our knees, and I felt as if I had
been tripped. I was up in a moment, however, but
she continued on her knees. I am sure she was pray-
ing, but very soon up she sprang. 'Oh, what is it,
what is it?' she cried; 'I must go to my father.'

"'I cannot tell you,' said I; 'I do not know, but
don't be frightened; how can such a little shock hurt
so big a ship?'

"It was all very well to tell her not to be fright-

ened, but when she ran below she left on deck about
as frightened a man as ever stood in shoes. There
could be no doubt about it; that horrible beast was
beginning to pull upon the ship. Whether or not it
would be able to draw us down below, was a question
which must soon be solved.

"I had had a small opinion of the maid, who, when
I told her the crew had deserted the ship, had sat
down and covered her head; but now I did pretty
much the same thing; I crouched on the deck and
pulled my cap over my eyes. I felt that I did not
wish to see, hear, or feel anything.

"I had sat in this way for about half an hour, and
had felt no more shocks, when a slight gurgling sound
came to my ears. I listened for a moment, then
sprang to my feet. Could we be moving? I ran to
the side of the ship. The gurgle seemed to be coming from the stern. I hurried there and looked over.
The wheel had been lashed fast, and the rudder stood
straight out behind us. On each side of it there was
a ripple in the quiet water. We were moving, and we
were moving backward!

"Overpowered by horrible fascination, I stood
grasping the rail, and looking over at the water beneath me, as the vessel moved slowly and steadily
onward, stern foremost. In spite of the upset condition of my mind, I could not help wondering why the
vessel should move in this way.

"There was only one explanation possible: The
Water-devil was walking along the bottom, and towing us after him! Why he should pull us along in

this way I could not imagine, unless he was making for his home in some dreadful cave at the bottom, into which he would sink, dragging us down after him.

"While my mind was occupied with these horrible subjects, some one touched me on the arm, and turning, I saw Miss Minturn. 'Are we not moving?' she said. 'Yes,' I answered, 'we certainly are.' 'Do you not think,' she then asked, 'that we may have been struck by a powerful current, which is now carrying us onward?' I did not believe this, for there was no reason to suppose that there were currents which wandered about, starting off vessels with a jerk, but I was glad to think that this idea had come into her head, and said that it was possible that this might be the case. 'And now we are going somewhere,' she said, speaking almost cheerfully. 'Yes, we are,' I answered, and I had to try hard not to groan as I said the words. 'And where do you think we are going?' she asked. It was altogether out of my power to tell that sweet creature that in my private opinion she, at least, was going to heaven, and so I answered that I really did not know. 'Well,' she said, 'if we keep moving, we're bound at last to get near land, or to some place where ships would pass near us.'

"There is nothing in this world," said the marine, "which does a man so much good in time of danger as to see a hopeful spirit in a woman — that is, a woman that he cares about. Some of her courage comes to him, and he is better and stronger for having her alongside of him."

Having made this remark, the speaker again glanced at the blacksmith's daughter. She had put down her work and was looking at him with an earnest brightness in her eyes.

"Yes," he continued, "it is astonishing what a change came over me, as I stood by the side of that noble girl. She was a born lady, I was a marine, just the same as we had been before, but there didn't seem to be the difference between us that there had been. Her words, her spirits, everything about her, in fact, seemed to act on me, to elevate me, to fill my soul with noble sentiments, to make another man of me. Standing there beside her, I felt myself her equal. In life or death I would not be ashamed to say, 'Here I am, ready to stand by you, whatever happens.'"

Having concluded this sentiment, the marine again glanced toward the blacksmith's daughter. Her eyes were slightly moist, and her face was glowing with a certain enthusiasm.

"Look here," said the blacksmith, "I suppose that woman goes along with you into the very maw of the sunken Devil, but I do wish you could take her more for granted, and get on faster with the real part of the story."

"One part is as real as another," said the marine; "but on we go, and on we did go for the whole of the rest of that day, at the rate of about half a knot an hour, as near as I could guess at it. The weather changed, and a dirty sort of fog came down on us, so that we couldn't see far in any direction.

"Why that Water-devil should keep on towing us,

and where he was going to take us, were things I
didn't dare to think about. The fog did not prevent
me from seeing the water about our stern, and I
leaned over the rail, watching the ripples that flowed
on each side of the rudder, which showed that we
were still going at about the same uniform rate.

"But toward evening the gurgling beneath me
ceased, and I could see that the rudder no longer
parted the quiet water, and that we had ceased to
move. A flash of hope blazed up within me. Had
the Water-devil found the ship too heavy a load, and
had he given up the attempt to drag it to its under-
ocean cave? I went below and had my supper; I
was almost a happy man. When Miss Minturn came
to ask me how we were getting along, I told her that
I thought we were doing very well indeed. I did not
mention that we had ceased to move, for she thought
that a favorable symptom. She went back to her
quarters greatly cheered up. Not so much, I think,
from my words, as from my joyful aspect; for I did
feel jolly, there was no doubt about it. If that Water-
devil had let go of us, I was willing to take all the
other chances that might befall a ship floating about
loose on the Bay of Bengal.

" The fog was so thick that night that it was damp
and unpleasant on deck, and so, having hung out and
lighted a couple of lanterns, I went below for a comfortable smoke in the captain's room. I was puffing
away here at my ease, with my mind filled with
happy thoughts of two or three weeks with Miss
Minturn on this floating paradise, where she was

bound to see a good deal of me, and couldn't help
liking me better, and depending on me more and
more every day, when I felt a little jerking shock.
It was the same thing that we had felt before. The
Water-devil still had hold of us!

"I dropped my pipe, my chin fell upon my breast,
I shivered all over. In a few moments I heard the
maid calling to me, and then she ran into the room.
'Miss Minturn wants to know, sir,' she said, 'if you
think that shock is a sudden twist in the current
which is carrying us on?' I straightened myself up
as well as I could, and in the dim light I do not think
she noticed my condition. I answered that I thought
it was something of that sort, and she went away.

"More likely, a twist of the Devil's arm, I thought,
as I sat there alone in my misery.

"In ten or fifteen minutes there came two shocks,
not very far apart. This showed that the creature
beneath us was at work in some way or another. Perhaps he had reached the opening of his den, and was
shortening up his arm before he plunged down into it
with us after him. I couldn't stay any longer in that
room alone. I looked for the maid, but she had put out
the galley light, and had probably turned in for the
night.

"I went up, and looked out on deck, but everything
was horribly dark and sticky and miserable there. I
noticed that my lanterns were not burning, and then
I remembered that I had not filled them. But this
did not trouble me. If a vessel came along and saw
our lights she would probably keep away from us, and

I would have been glad to have a vessel come to us,
even if she ran into us.   Our steamer would probably
float long enough for us to get on board the other one,
and almost anything would be better than being left
alone in this dreadful place, at the mercy of the
Water-devil.

"Before I left the deck I felt another shock.   This
took out of me whatever starch was left, and I shuffled below and got to my bunk, where I tumbled in
and covered myself up, head and all.   If there had
been any man to talk to, it would have been different,
but I don't know when I ever felt more deserted than
I did at that time.

"I tried to forget the awful situation in which I
was; I tried to think of other things; to imagine that
I was drilling with the rest of my company, with Tom
Rogers on one side of me, and old Humphrey Peters
on the other.   You may say, perhaps, that this wasn't
exactly the way of carrying out my promise of taking
care of Miss Minturn and the others.   But what was
there to do?   When the time came to do anything,
and I could see what to do, I was ready to do it; but
there was no use of waking them up now and setting
their minds on edge, when they were all comfortable
in their beds, thinking that every jerk of the Devil's
arm was a little twist in the current that was carrying
them to Calcutta or some other desirable port.

"I felt some shocks after I got into bed, but whether
or not there were many in the night, I don't know, for
I went to sleep.   It was daylight when I awoke, and
jumping out of my bunk I dashed on deck.   Every-

thing seemed pretty much as it had been, and the fog
was as thick as ever. I ran to the stern and looked
over, and I could scarcely believe my eyes when I saw
that we were moving again, still stern foremost, but a
little faster than before. That beastly Water-devil
had taken a rest for the night, and had probably given
us the shocks by turning over in his sleep, and now he
was off again, making up for lost time.

"Pretty soon Miss Minturn came on deck, and bade
me good morning, and then she went and looked over
the stern. 'We are still moving on,' she said, with a
smile, 'and the fog doesn't seem to make any difference. It surely cannot be long before we get somewhere.' 'No, miss,' said I, 'it cannot be very long.'
'You look tired,' she said, 'and I don't wonder, for you
must feel the heavy responsibility on you. I have
told my maid to prepare breakfast for you in our
cabin. I want my father to know you, and I think it
is a shame that you, the only protector that we have,
should be shut off so much by yourself; so after this
we shall eat together.' 'After this,' I groaned to myself, 'we shall be eaten together.' At that moment I did
not feel that I wanted to breakfast with Miss Minturn."

"Mr. Cardly," said Mr. Harberry to the school-
master, "have you ever read, in any of your scientific
books, that the Bay of Bengal is subject to heavy fogs
that last day after day ? "

"I cannot say," answered the school-master, "that
my researches into the geographical distribution of
fogs have resulted — "

"As to fogs," interrupted the marine, "you can't

get rid of them, you know. If you had been in the habit of going to sea, you would know that you are likely to run into a fog at any time, and in any weather; and as to lasting, they are just as likely to last for days as for hours. It wasn't the fog that surprised me. I did not consider that of any account at all. I had enough other things to occupy my mind." And having settled this little matter, he went on with his story.

"Well, my friends, I did not breakfast with Miss Minturn and her father. Before that meal was ready, and while I was standing alone at the stern, I saw coming out of the water, a long way off in the fog, which must have been growing thinner about this time, a dark and mysterious object, apparently without any shape or form. This sight made the teeth chatter in my head. I had expected to be pulled down to the Water-devil, but I had never imagined that he would come up to us!

"While my eyes were glued upon this apparition, I could see that we were approaching it. When I perceived this, I shut my eyes and turned my back — I could look upon it no longer. My mind seemed to forsake me; I did not even try to call out and give the alarm to the others. Why should I? What could they do?"

"If it had been me," said Mrs. Fryker, in a sort of gasping whisper, "I should have died right there." The marine turned his eyes in the direction of the blacksmith's daughter. She was engaged with her work, and was not looking at him.

"I cannot say," he continued, "that, had Miss Minturn been there at that moment, that I would not have declared that I was ready to die for her or with her; but there was no need of trying to keep up her courage, that was all right. She knew nothing of our danger. That terrible knowledge pressed on me alone. Is it wonderful that a human soul should sink a little under such an awful load?" Without turning to observe the effect of these last words, the marine went on. "Suddenly I heard behind me a most dreadful sound. 'Good Heavens,' I exclaimed, 'can a Water-devil bray?'

"The sound was repeated. Without knowing what I did, I turned. I heard what sounded like words; I saw in the fog the stern of a vessel, with a man above it, shouting to me through a speaking-trumpet.

"I do not know what happened next; my mind must have become confused. When I regained my senses, Miss Minturn, old Mr. Minturn, and the maid were standing by me. The man had stopped shouting from his trumpet, and a boat was being lowered from the other ship. In about ten minutes there were half-a-dozen men on board of us, all in the uniform of the British navy. I was stiff enough now, and felt myself from top to toe a regular marine in the service of my country. I stepped up to the officer in command and touched my cap.

"He looked at me and my companions in surprise, and then glancing along the deck, said, 'What has happened to this vessel? Who is in command?' I informed him, that, strictly speaking, no one was in command, but that I represented the captain, officers, and crew of this steamer, the *General Brooks,* from San Francisco to Calcutta, and I then proceeded to tell him the whole story of our misfortunes; and concluded by telling the officer, that if we had not moved since his vessel had come in sight, it was probably because the Water-devil had let go of us, and was preparing to make fast to the other ship; and therefore it would be advisable for us all to get on board his vessel, and steam away as quickly as possible.

"The Englishmen looked at me in amazement. 'Drunk!' ejaculated the officer I had addressed. 'Cracked, I should say,' suggested another. 'Now,' spoke up Mr. Minturn, 'I do not understand what I have just heard,' he said. 'What is a Water-devil? I am astounded.' 'You never said a word of this to me!' exclaimed Miss Minturn. 'You never told me that we were in the grasp of a Water-devil, and that that was the reason the captain and the crew ran away.' 'No,' said I, 'I never divulged the dreadful danger we were in. I allowed you to believe that we were in the influence of a current, and that the shocks we felt were the sudden twists of that current. The terrible truth I kept to myself. Not for worlds would I have made known to a tenderly nurtured lady, to her invalid father, and devoted servant, what might have crushed their souls, driven them to the borders of frenzy; in which case the relief which now has come to us would have been of no avail.'

"The officer stood and steadily stared at me. 'I declare,' he said, 'you do not look like a crazy man.

At what time did this Water-devil begin to take you in tow?'

"'Yesterday morning,' I answered. 'And he stopped during last night?' he asked. I replied that that was the case. Then he took off his cap, rubbed his head, and stood silent for a minute. 'We'll look into this matter!' he suddenly exclaimed, and turning, he and his party left us to ourselves. The boat was now sent back with a message to the English vessel, and the officers and men who remained scattered themselves over our steamer, examining the engine-room, hold, and every part of her.

"I was very much opposed to all this delay; for although the Englishmen might doubt the existence of the Water-devil, I saw no reason to do so, and in any case I was very anxious to be on the safe side by getting away as soon as possible; but, of course, British officers would not be advised by me, and as I was getting very hungry I went down to breakfast. I ate this meal alone, for my fellow-passengers seemed to have no desire for food.

"I cannot tell all that happened during the next hour, for, to tell the truth, I did not understand everything that was done. The boat passed several times between the two vessels, bringing over a number of men—two of them scientific fellows, I think. Another was a diver, whose submarine suit and air-pumping machines came over with him. He was lowered over the side, and after he had been down about fifteen minutes he was hauled up again, and down below was the greatest hammering and hauling that ever you heard. The *General Brooks* was put in charge of an officer and some men; a sail was hoisted to keep her in hand, so that she wouldn't drift into the other ship; and in the midst of all the rowdy-dow we were told that if we liked we might go on board the English vessel immediately.

"Miss Minturn and her party instantly accepted this invitation, and although under ordinary circumstances I would have remained to see for myself what these people found out, I felt a relief in the thought of leaving that vessel which is impossible for me to express, and I got into the boat with the others.

"We were treated very handsomely on board the English vessel, which was a mail steamship, at that time in the employment of the English Government. I told my story at least half-a-dozen times, sometimes to the officers and sometimes to the men, and whether they believed me or not, I don't think any one ever created a greater sensation with a story of the sea.

"In an hour or so the officer in charge of the operations on the *General Brooks* came aboard. As he passed me on his way to the captain, he said, 'We found your Water-devil, my man.' 'And he truly had us in tow?' I cried. 'Yes, you are perfectly correct,' he said, and went on to make his report to the captain."

"Now, then," said the blacksmith, "I suppose we are going to get to the pint. What did he report?"

"I didn't hear his report," said the marine, "but everybody soon knew what had happened to our unlucky vessel, and I can give you the whole story of it.

The *General Brooks* sailed from San Francisco to Calcutta, with a cargo of stored electricity, contained in
large, strongly made boxes. This I knew nothing
about, not being in the habit of inquiring into cargoes. Well, in some way or other, which I don't
understand, not being a scientific man myself, a magnetic connection was formed between these boxes, and
also, if I got the story straight, between them and the
iron hull of our vessel, so that it became, in fact, an
enormous floating magnet, one of the biggest things of
the kind on record. I have an idea that this magnetic
condition was the cause of the trouble to our machinery; every separate part of it was probably turned
to a magnet, and they all stuck together."

"Mr. Cardly," said Mr. Harberry to the school-
master, "I do not suppose you have given much attention to the study of commerce, and therefore are
not prepared to give us any information in regard to
stored electricity as an article of export from this
country; but perhaps you can tell us what stored electricity is, and how it is put into boxes."

"In regard to the transportation," answered the
school-master, speaking a little slowly, "of encased
electric potency, I cannot — "

"Oh, bless me!" interrupted the marine; "that is all
simple enough; you can store electricity and send it
all over the world, if you like; in places like Calcutta,
I think it must be cheaper to buy it than to make it.
They use it as a motive power for sewing-machines,
apple-parers, and it can be used in a lot of ways, such
as digging post-holes and churning butter. When the

stored electricity in a box is all used up, all you have
to do is to connect a fresh box with your machinery,
and there you are, ready to start again. There was
nothing strange about our cargo. It was the electricity leaking out and uniting itself and the iron ship
into a sort of conglomerate magnet that was out of
the way."

"Mr. Cardly," said Mr. Harberry, "if an iron ship
were magnetized in that manner, wouldn't it have a
deranging effect upon the needle of the compass?"

The marine did not give the school-master time to
make answer. "Generally speaking," said he, "that
sort of thing would interfere with keeping the vessel
on its proper course, but with us it didn't make any
difference at all. The greater part of the ship was in
front of the binnacle where they keep the compass,
and so the needle naturally pointed that way, and as
we were going north before a south wind, it was all
right.

"Being a floating magnet, of course, did not prevent our sailing, so we went along well enough until
we came to longitude 90°, latitude 15° north. Now
it so happened that a telegraphic cable which had
been laid down by the British Government to estab-
lish communication between Madras and Rangoon,
had broken some time before, and not very far from
this point.

"Now you can see for yourselves that when an
enormous mass of magnetic iron, in the shape of
the *General Brooks*, came sailing along there, the
part of that cable which lay under us was so attracted

by such a powerful and irresistible force that its
broken end raised itself from the bottom of the bay
and reached upward until it touched our ship, when
it laid itself along our keel, to which it instantly became fastened as firmly as if it had been bolted and
riveted there. Then, as the rest of this part of the
cable was on the bottom of the bay all the way to
Madras, of course we had to stop; that's simple
enough. That's the way the Water-devil held us fast
in one spot for two days.

"The British Government determined not to repair
this broken cable, but to take it up and lay down a
better one; so they chartered a large steamer, and
fitted her up with engines, and a big drum that they
use for that sort of thing, and set her to work to
wind up the Madras end of the broken cable. She
had been at this business a good while before we
were caught by the other end, and when they got
near enough to us for their engines to be able to
take up the slack from the bottom between us and
them, then of course they pulled upon us, and we
began to move. And when they lay to for the
night, and stopped the winding business, of course
we stopped, and the stretch of cable between the two
ships had no effect upon us, except when the big mail
steamer happened to move this way or that, as they
kept her head to the wind; and that's the way we lay
quiet all night except when we got our shocks.

"When they set the drum going again in the
morning, it wasn't long before they wound us near
. enough for them to see us, which they would have

done sooner if my lights hadn't gone out so early in the evening."

"And that," said the blacksmith, with a somewhat severe expression on his face, "is all that you have to tell about your wonderful Water-devil!"

"All!" said the marine; "I should say it was quite enough, and nothing could be more wonderful than what really happened. A Water-devil is one of two things: he is real, or he's not real. If he's not real, he's no more than an ordinary spook or ghost, and is not to be practically considered. If he's real, then he's an alive animal, and can be put in a class with other animals, and described in books, because even if nobody sees him, the scientific men know how he must be constructed, and then he's no more than a great many other wonderful things, which we can see alive, stuffed, or in plaster casts.

"But if you want to put your mind upon something really wonderful, just think of a snake-like rope of wire, five or six hundred miles long, lying down at the very bottom of the great Bay of Bengal, with no more life in it than there is in a ten-penny nail.

"Then imagine that long, dead wire snake to be suddenly filled with life, and to know that there was something far up above it, on the surface of the water, that it wants to reach up to and touch. Think of it lifting and flapping its broken end, and then imagine it raising yard after yard of itself up and up, through the solemn water, more and more of it lifting itself from the bottom, curling itself backward and forward as it rises higher and higher, until at

last, with a sudden jump that must have ripped a
mile or more of it from the bottom, it claps its end
against the thing it wants to touch, and which it can
neither see, nor hear, nor smell, but which it knows
is there. Could there be anything in this world more
wonderful than that?

"And then, if that isn't enough of a wonder, think
of the Rangoon end of that cable squirming and wrig-
gling and stretching itself out toward our ship, but
not being able to reach us on account of a want of
slack; just as alive as the Madras part of the cable,
and just as savage and frantic to get up to us and lay
hold of us; and then, after our vessel had been gradually pulled away from it, think of this other part getting weaker and weaker, minute by minute, until it
falls flat on the bay, as dead as any other iron
thing!"

The marine ceased to speak, and Mrs. Fryker
heaved a sigh.

"It makes me shiver to think of all that down so
deep," she said; "but I must say I am disappointed."

"In what way?" asked the marine.

"A Water-devil," said she, "as big as six whales,
and with a funnelly mouth to suck in people, is different; but, of course, after all, it was better as it was."

"Look here," said the blacksmith, "what became
of the girl? I wanted her finished up long ago, and
you haven't done it yet."

"Miss Minturn, you mean," said the marine.
"Well, there is not much to say about her. Things
happened in the usual way. When the danger was

all over, when she had other people to depend upon
besides me, and we were on board a fine steamer, with
a lot of handsomely dressed naval officers, and going
comfortably to Madras, of course she thought no more
of the humble sea-soldier who once stood between her
and — nobody knew what. In fact, the only time she
spoke to me after we got on board the English
steamer, she made me feel, although she didn't say
it in words, that she was not at all obliged to me for
supposing that she would have been scared to death
if I had told her about the Water-devil."

"I suppose," said the blacksmith, "by the time
you got back to your ship you had overstayed your
leave of absence a good while. Did your captain let
you off when you told him this story of the new-
fashioned Water-devil?"

The marine smiled. "I never went back to the
*Apache*," he said. "When I arrived at Madras I
found that she had sailed from Calcutta. It was, of
course, useless for me to endeavor to follow her, and
I therefore concluded to give up the marine service
for a time and go into another line of business, about
which it is too late to tell you now."

"Mr. Cardly," said Mr. Harberry to the school-
master, "have you ever read that the British Government has a submarine cable from Madras to
Rangoon?"

The marine took it upon himself to answer this
question. "The cable of which I spoke to you," he
said, "was taken up, as I told you, and I never heard
that another one was laid. But it is getting late, and

I think I will go to bed; I have a long walk before me to-morrow." So saying he rose, put his pipe upon the mantel-piece, and bade the company good night. As he did so, he fixed his eyes on the blacksmith's daughter, but that young lady did not look at him; she was busily reading the weekly newspaper, which her father had left upon the table.

Mr. Harberry now rose, preparatory to going home; and as he buttoned up his coat, he looked from one to another of the little group, and remarked, "I have often heard that marines are a class of men who are considered as fit subjects to tell tough stories to, but it strikes me that the time has come when the tables are beginning to be turned."

Typography by J. S. Cushing & Co., Boston.

Presswork by Berwick & Smith, Boston.

www.ingramcontent.com/pod-product-compliance
Lightning Source LLC
Chambersburg PA
CBHW032005240626
47153CB00003B/1133